Daughters and Destinies

ALSO BY INDOO SETH

Emotional Hostage (2015)

Love Laws & Outlaws (2016)

daughters

and

destinies

~ a novel ~

INDOO SETH

TIGER PRINT

SPEAKING TIGER PUBLISHING PVT. LTD
4381/4, Ansari Road, Daryaganj
New Delhi 110002

First published in Tiger Print by Speaking Tiger 2019

ISBN: 978-93-88874-62-5
eISBN: 978-93-88874-57-1

10 9 8 7 6 5 4 3 2 1

Typeset in Sabon LT Std by SÜRYA, New Delhi
Printed at Sanat Printers, Kundli

To Salamat, Rajni and Khushi.
How easy and comfortable they have made
my life over the years.

1

On the day that Ram died the monsoons had just arrived in Delhi.

Strong winds were blowing all the leaves that had gathered on the driveway when Mamta stepped out from her employers' bungalow on Aurangzeb Road in the evening, after finishing her day's work. The sky was overcast and the first light rain was beginning to fall on the parched earth. The fresh smell and feel of the rain brought a smile to Mamta's lips. It always took her back to her childhood, when she would pine for the monsoons to arrive and end the torrid heat of summer. With the first drops falling on the ground, she would run out of her hut and dance, looking up at the sky and thanking the gods for washing away the sins of the past year.

Mamta was twenty-two years old and moderately overweight after Ranju's birth, unable to shed her extra kilos. She had a glowing, dusky complexion and her beaming eyes revealed a rare contentment. Mamta was no beauty, but she had an infectiously positive energy and a contagious smile that made men look at her, and then look again. She was an amiable woman, compassionate and habitually prone to helping others. Her genial nature won her immense popularity in the DID Colony slum she lived in.

At the gate of Mrs Sareen's sprawling bungalow the guard, Vijay, offered her an umbrella but she refused it with a smile. She loved feeling the tingle of raindrops on her skin. Looking up at the leaden sky, she knew it was going to pour heavily. She stopped by the vegetable vendor on her way home to buy some eggplant and a can of mustard oil. The thought of her husband, Ram, brought a smile to her face. He relished her baingan bharta, calling it 'the food of the Gods'. He would beg her to make it almost every week. She decided to surprise him and cook it again tonight. Mamta loved Ram and eagerly waited to spend time with him at the end of every day. Ram was a kind and affable man who would massage her aching feet as they talked. He took great pride in feeding Ranju, their two-year-old daughter. Every Sunday, both father and daughter would impatiently wait for the chicken meal she cooked for lunch on her day off. Ram was an electrician and he enjoyed spending Sundays at home, unless there was an urgent call from one of his favourite clients.

As Mamta walked home, the rain grew heavier and lightning split the sky, making her regret not accepting the umbrella from Vijay. She wondered if Gita and Ranju were waiting for her, and whether Ram might be hurrying to meet her at her Mrs Sareen's with an umbrella.

When Mamta returned from work each day, she would have no time for anyone but her family. Ranju would become her priority and cooking for Ram gave her much joy. Mamata had married Ram when she was barely nineteen. They were from the same village in Bhojpur, Bihar, and had come to Delhi with dreams of making a better future. They had been neighbours in their village and had known each other since they were children. Ram had secretly loved her throughout, and had coaxed his parents into arranging their marriage. He was an ambitious man and his love for Mamta invigorated his ambition. Their relationship was built on trust and respect, which had become stronger with every passing year.

They moved to Delhi soon after their marriage and little Ranju was born eleven months later. Ram encouraged Mamta to take up a job as a domestic cleaner in order to increase their earnings and save adequately for the future. Their aim was to make sure that Ranju got a good education in a private school. Ram and Mamta had known poverty in the village and understood the disadvantages they had suffered.

Ram was a good-looking Bihari: tall, fair and confident. He always kept his thick black hair generously oiled and swept back from his broad forehead. He believed that this was a sign of intelligence. He was slim and athletic, although he had never played any sport in his life. He liked wearing crisp white shirts tucked neatly into his trousers and his only pair of shoes was always well polished. His obvious pride in himself and his honesty gave him an edge over his colleagues.

Ranju was a talkative and enthusiastic child. Her mop

of black curls framed an oval face with innocent, curious eyes. Her eagerness to learn was a perennial source of pleasure to her parents. Every week, Ram brought Ranju picture books to encourage her to read. One day, Ram and Mamta laughed uproariously when she tried to nibble at them. Ranju was the apple of their eye.

Mamta's best friend, Gita, lived in the next lane of DID Colony. Gita was a home-maker, while her husband, Jagdish, earned well as the cook of a Supreme Court judge. The judge believed that everyone deserved a good education and paid the school fees of Gita and Jagdish's two sons. So Gita had volunteered to look after Ranju while Mamta was at work. Gita would attend to Ranju from eleven to six every day after Ram left for work late in the morning. Every evening Gita, with Ranju in her arms, would wait for Mamta at the top of the road that led to DID Colony. They would walk home together, chit-chatting and catching up. Their five minutes of daily gossip was an important source of entertainment and information for Mamta. Mamta insisted on paying Gita, but Gita had grown to love Ranju like her own daughter and refused to accept any money. Mamta, however, would just embrace her and leave the money on her kitchen table.

Gita secretly admired the love that Mamta and Ram shared. She was ten years older than Mamta and treated her like a younger sister. She was unusually tall and her broad frame made her look masculine. Her hair was always tied neatly in a bun on top of her head, which added to her already imposing height. No one in the slum dared to mess with Gita. She had a slight limp in her walk and the children in the slum often mimicked her behind her back. If she caught any child poking fun she would chase after them with a stick till her legs gave way.

Although Jagdish was afraid of his wife, Gita took inordinate pride in her husband's job, never missing an opportunity to boast about the judge's lavish bungalow, his power and influence. She was indignant about her neighbours going to sweep people's homes and often deliberated over it with Jagdish, who secretly hoped his wife would work too. However Gita openly expressed her distaste for such work, lamenting that her only friend in the colony was a safaiwali. Mamta would explain that they had moved to the city to make a better future, but Gita would insist that it was the man's responsibility to look after his family and meet its needs. They argued on and off about their different values, but grew to love each other immensely.

Wet from the rain, Mamta finally reached Gita's shanty at 6:30. 'Ma!' screamed little Ranju and ran to hug her mother, leaving the banana she was eating on the floor. Mamta picked her up, tightly embracing her and showering her with kisses.

'I missed you, Ranju! Let's go home. Today I'm going to cook Papa's favourite baingan bharta and some kheer for my dear daughter.'

'Why didn't you wait for the rain to stop, Mamta? You will get sick!' Gita said, handing her a towel.

'Thanks, Gita…I wanted to reach home and finish

cooking. Ram should be home any minute now,' Mamta replied as she took Ranju and hurried towards her house.

By this time, the rain had stopped. Mamta crossed the street to reach her shack. Looking down the lane she smiled when she saw little children running around, dripping wet and squealing in delight. Mamta marvelled at how children were able to find pleasure from small things. But her momentary joy soon turned to anxiety: was her little Ranju going to grow up like them?

When she got home she saw that the asbestos roof had started to leak again and rainwater had begun to seep in through the walls. If this went on, Mamta feared the roof would cave in on them some day while sleeping. This fear haunted her like a bad dream, and she vowed to take it up again with Ram. She had argued with him several times, but Ram had different concerns.

'Do you have any idea how much it will cost us?' he asked her, more than once, in a gently mocking tone.

'I want us to be safe, that's all,' Mamta would cry.

Ram would then placate her and promise to buy some new roofing sheets the moment they had saved a little money.

Was she going to end the day arguing with Ram again over the leaking roof? Why couldn't he just understand? For the moment, she had to get out of her wet clothes without delay before she caught a cold. She placed Ranju on the bed and wiped her messy hands, which were sticky from the banana she had been eating at Gita's house. She left the door to the hut open wanting some fresh air. She drew the curtain that ran along the back wall to give herself some privacy to get into some dry clothes. But Ranju jumped off the bed and followed her behind the curtain. Mamta burst out laughing.

'Ranju, let Ma change before she catches a cold. Go sit on the bed and I'll give you your colouring book in a minute.' Ranju, not letting go of her mother, stared up at her with a frown. Mamta couldn't resist giving her a kiss on her lips but then she pushed her out. Glancing at the watch lying in the alcove, cluttered with her and Ram's personal belongings, while changing, she felt lucky to have enough room in their house. It was already 6:20 pm. Ram should have been home by now, she thought. He must have got caught in the rain too. She stepped out from behind the curtain and pulled out a colouring book and colour pencils from a small carton in the corner.

'I want to watch TV, Ma,' Ranju said. Their 14-inch black and white TV, a new acquisition, was set on two aluminium boxes placed one on top of the other. All Ranju wished for was to watch TV when either of her parents were home.

'No, Ranju, not now. We'll watch your favourite cartoon programme after dinner, promise. Papa should be home any minute so let me make some dinner quickly. You know how hungry he gets after work.'

Mamta rolled out a yoga mat which her employer had given her and opened up Ranju's colouring book. 'Come, sit here and wait for Papa. I'll get started on dinner.'

Ranju obediently did as she was told. Mamta hurriedly opened the small fridge to take out the leftover rotis from the morning. Ram usually preferred eating his dinner early so he could spend time playing with Ranju or walking her to the nearby ice-cream vendor. Mamta sat down on a low stool by the two-burner stove, pulled out the baingan from the plastic bag and placed it on the fire. The heat from the stove forced her to switch on the small table fan next to her. The need for a new fan was urgent but it would have to wait. At work, Ram's ambition drove him to come up with innovative ideas. He had frequently asked his clients to take pictures of the wiring before the drywall went up in their houses, to able them to track electrical placements in the future. His work with Diwali lights left his customers spellbound and their respect for him grew over the years. He was the most sought after electrician in the area. Mamta reached out for the pakkad, neatly placed on a newspaper next to the stove, evenly roasting the eggplant.

The jerry can in the corner was only half-filled with water. She hadn't had enough time in the morning to refill it. She would ask Ram to do so before they turned in for the day. The stale smell from unwashed dishes would give her a sleepless night. She usually filled her jerry can early in the morning and used the water for cooking, washing utensils and bathing Ranju. There was also a pile of unwashed clothes lying in a bucket, but she decided to wait for the rains to clear. Mamta preferred to keep her room as tidy as possible, which at times was impractical with Ranju.

She looked at her watch again: it was 6:45. What was keeping Ram? she wondered. Continuing to roast the eggplant, she looked at Ranju bent over, engrossed in colouring a black bird.

With a smile Mamta walked over and pulling her cheek she asked, 'Is that a crow you are trying to colour, Ranju?' Ranju nodded but did not look up.

With a tender pat on her head, Mamta turned back to the stove. The eggpant was almost done, so she began chopping onions, tomatoes, green chillies and coriander leaves for the tadka, before adding the mashed eggplant. As she sat before the stove she began once more to wonder when they would have a small house of their own. She had to persuade Ram, she realized, to take a loan and buy a fifty-square-meter plot on the outskirts of Delhi.

The slum was becoming more congested day by day. With the increasing number of people moving in, the huts were crammed together like matchsticks in a matchbox. It was difficult to step out for fresh air. It seemed like the earth beneath their feet was shrinking. From thirty huts in the past, there were now more than fifty and the living conditions were deplorable. While chopping the onions she toyed with the idea of working in a pickle factory in order to earn more. Her innate optimism gave her the power to dream, but reality would then remind her that she was an uneducated and unskilled woman who couldn't even read. The truth would sadden her till her natural optimism reasserted itself.

The bharta was ready at last, and as she warmed the

rotis on the stove, Mamta wiped her sweaty neck with the end of her saree. Once finished, Mamta piled the rotis in a small tiffin box, keeping it close to the stove and warm.

Glancing at the watch again, she felt the first touch of irritation with Ram for being so late. Normally, he would walk in even before she began to cook dinner. Ranju had dozed off on the mat.

Standing up to wash her hands and put her daughter on the bed, she saw Gita standing at the door. Her face was streaming with tears, her lips quivering, but not a word escaped her mouth.

'What happened, didi? Have you had a fight with Jagdish bhai?'

Gita crossed over to her swiftly and hugged her. Her behaviour was odd and Mamta could sense something was wrong. The words that had been dammed up inside Gita began to burst forth, but she kept stuttering and crying.

'Ram Bhai...gone... Ram Bhai gone... Gone!'

'Where?' asked Mamta, trying to keep an eye on Ranju so she wouldn't slip off the bed.

'No, he has left us. He has left us...'

Unable to understand, Mamta felt a pang of dread. In a voice crackling with anger she demanded, 'What rubbish are you speaking?'

Unwittingly, she approached Gita, her hand raised as if to hit her. But Gita sank to the ground and began to sob hysterically.

'Ram is no more. Jagdish... couldn't save him. He tried and tried, but he just...couldn't.'

Ram was dead. An unbearable pain which she had never known before ballooned in Mamta as she registered what her friend was trying to say. Death had come, suddenly, and taken her love, her breadwinner, her life, her happiness away from her, forever. As she held on to the the door of her hut, Mamta could feel her body turning to water.

'Where is he?' she managed to say.

'Under the neem tree,' Gita said between sobs.

Mamta ran out to the neem tree and stood looking at Ram's lifeless body. Tears fell from her eyes in an endless stream. She knelt beside his body, touching his hand, refusing to accept the cruel reality of his end. His body was still warm. She put her ear to his heart, hoping to hear a faint sound. She kept caressing his face and kissing his forehead.

'Wake up, Ram!' she screamed. 'What will I tell Ranju? You can't do this to me.'

Jagdish signalled to Gita to take Mamta away till she regained her composure. Gita started pulling Mamta away gently, but Mamta tore herself away and fell upon Ram's body, resting her head on his chest and sobbing inconsolably. Her pain grew and grew till she felt her heart was on fire. The world shrank to a burning point. Mercifully she slipped into unconsciousness.

Gita signalled to a couple of the women who had gathered around Ram's body to help her carry Mamta back to her shanty. Ranju could not be left alone and required attention too. Gita ran ahead of Mamta to her shanty, picked up Ranju, who had just awoken, held her tight and hurried to her house before she could see her mother's plight. Gita's sons took over, giving Ranju her dinner and putting her to bed. Gita, devastated herself, kept shunting between the two shanties to make sure both Mamta and Ranju were well attended to. The last thing she needed was for Ranju to wake up and look for her parents.

Mamta was restless all night, tossing and turning in her semi-conscious state. She would stretch out her hand every now and again, hoping to find Ram lying next to her, sit up looking stunned, and begin to cry again till exhaustion took her and led her back into restless sleep. Sitting beside her, Gita could not stop thinking about what Jagdish had told her.

That evening, after the storm had subsided, Jagdish had decided to cycle home in the drizzle and rest for an hour, before going back to work. It was going to be a long night for him as his employers were expecting friends for dinner. Like the rest of the residents of DID Colony who worked on the other side of Lodhi gardens, Jagdish used the narrow bicycle path as a shortcut. Shortly after he entered the park he saw a group of people further ahead. From a distance, Jagdish could see that a bulky branch had fallen across the path. A small crowd was gathering and a couple of people were trying to lift it and push it to one side. Coming closer, Jagdish realized they were trying to rescue a man who was trapped beneath the branch. Unable to lift the heavy log, they started breaking smaller branches to clear the way. When he heard the man groaning in pain he immediately got off his bicycle, parked it on one side and went to help.

The storm began to intensify and the sky darkened. Fearing that another branch might fall and hurt someone else, a few people in the crowd began to slip away. The trapped man continued to groan but his groans were getting weaker. Jagdish pulled out his mobile phone and flashed the torch light, but it wasn't much help. So he dialled 100 for the police. As they waited for the police to arrive the squall passed. The crowd swelled once more, but still couldn't lift the thick branch. Rolling it off was not an option as it would have crushed the man beneath it.

Acknowledging defeat, everyone settled down around the tree in silence, not knowing what else to do. Jagdish had never experienced such helplessness and despair. The man's groans became less audible and subsided into a whisper. 'Help me, help me,' was all he could manage to say. There was nothing anyone could do but look at each other and wait. It was forty minutes before the crane arrived. By then the whispers had ceased.

It was only when the crane lifted the branch and Jagdish was able to approach the injured man that he realized he was looking at Ram's lifeless face. Paralyzed by shock, it took him a whole five minutes before he could gather himself and identify Ram for the police. The officer present made Jagdish sign a declaration of 'Death by Accident' and brought Ram's body back to the slum with the help of a small group of passersby. As they laid his body below the neem tree, the slum-dwellers surrounded his corpse, totally dumbstruck.

'Go, bring Mamta,' one of the elders said. But Jagdish asked them to fetch Gita instead.

'We will have to break it to her slowly," he said.

Gita was cooking her evening meal when she was informed of the sad news. Numbed with shock she rushed out and ran straight to the neem tree.

When Jagdish put his arm around her shoulders she collapsed next to it. 'Go bring Mamta. You are her closest friend, she must hear this from you.'

Gita covered her face with both her hands and went running to Mamta's shanty. Gita knew how much the couple loved each other and how difficult it would be for Mamta to live alone. Thousands of such little worries ran through Gita's mind. But she had to do the inevitable, she had to tell Mamta she had lost Ram forever.

The next day, with the coming of dawn it became necessary to prepare for Ram's cremation. Mamta, still under the neem tree, kept a tight grip on Ram's arm, not letting go.

'Let go, Mamta! We have to prepare Ram for the cremation,' Jagdish told her firmly.

Cremation. The awful finality of the word brought her out of her stupor.

Reluctantly she released her grip. 'Take her back home,' Jagdish told Gita. 'I and the other men will bathe and dress Ram.'

Gita went back to her hut with Mamta to find Ranju still asleep. 'Let her stay with me for a couple of days,' said Gita, gently placing her hand on Ranju's head, as Mamta simply nodded without any expression, her face drained of any life.

2

For the next few weeks, Mamta sat hunched in her hut, unable to cope with the finality of Ram's death. Ranju was often dazed when her mother would suddenly break out into uncontrolled, loud sobbing. The little girl would silently slink into a corner watching her, never daring to ask where her father was.

Although Ranju had been asleep when they brought Ram home, her little brain had soon deciphered that something was very wrong. She missed her father's lap, their weekend outings and the picture books he bought for her. She was bored of flipping over the same pages over and over again. Her only consolation was that her mother no longer went to work, and she was around the whole time.

There were days when she would slip away and spend hours with Gita aunty in her shack. She adored and loved her Gita aunty, who often walked her to the ice-cream vendor for an orange bar. And Jagdish Uncle just yesterday had bought her a colouring book and some new colour pencils to keep her occupied.

'Why is Ma crying all the time? And where is

Papa?' she would ask Gita, her eyes begging for an explanation.

But Gita had no ready answers. Pointing her finger towards the sky, she would try to reassure little Ranju. 'Papa is with God. You are a good girl and he is happy to see you from there.'

'When will he come back? I miss him and Ma misses him too.'

Looking into Ranju's dewy eyes Gita felt helpless. She had nothing to say to a little girl who couldn't yet understand death. She would just hug her or distract her with some inane conversation.

Unable to understand how everything had changed so drastically in their lives, Ranju gradually retreated into a shell of her own. She longed for her mother's affectionate hugs and kisses, the chicken meals on Sunday and the bicycle rides with her father to the vegetable market. Her mother would just make parathas most of the time, without any vegetables or dal. She no longer forced Ranju to finish her meals. She would forget to bathe her till the smell from Ranju's clothes helped her recall her duty. Ranju now looked like a dirty, scruffy child who hadn't had her hair combed or washed in weeks.

Mamta's mother and brother came to Delhi from Bihar, staying with her for a month, but they had to get back as the paddy transplanting had begun. They offered to take Mamta back to the village but she refused to go. For another month Mamta stayed in her hut: crying whenever a new memory of Ram and their lost happinness bit into her, eating whatever Gita brought for her and Ranju. She stopped working. Gita helped her out in running the house whenever she could.

This could not go on forever. Finally, one evening Gita chastised her friend, trying to remind her of her duty as a mother. 'You have to pull yourself out of your misery, Mamta, and take care of your daughter. I'm doing as much as I can, but she needs the love of her mother. She's crawling into a shell and hardly talks to any of us. My boys try and distract her but she is lost and confused. You have to get a grip on yourself, Mamta, and face the future.'

Gita knew she was hurting Mamta, but her heart bled every time she saw little Ranju with a vacant look in her eyes, not willing to leave her hut or play with other children. Every time someone came over, Ranju would excitedly rush to the door, hoping it would be her Papa, and then turn away heartbroken. Imitating her parents, she often stood before the idols with folded hands and muttered her own little prayer when nobody was around. Meanwhile Mamta was still in shock. She was scared for their future. Gita could only helplessly wish for them to start leading a healthy life again.

With every passing day Mamta looked thinner and lifeless. She walked sluggishly and her gaunt face frightened her too, when she chanced upon it in the mirror. She now had deep lines on either side of her lips and she couldn't make eye contact with anyone. She would speak with her eyes fixed on the ground. People in the slum began to avoid her, afraid she would burst into tears.

Life without Ram was meaningless. The single room of her hut constantly reminded her of him. Memories of her lost happiness haunted her soul and she had lost the desire to look after Ranju. Ranju often fell asleep without even eating her dinner. The nights were a time of terror for Mamta, who would lie awake trembling at the thought of their uncertain future. She had to make her own arrangements, pay her rent and look after Ranju. The memory of Ram lying lifeless in the courtyard under the neem tree would return to haunt her again and again.

One morning Mamta was lying down on her bed facing the wall, tightly hugging her pillow, when she heard an ear-piercing scream. She got up to see her daughter sitting by the stove, with her foot covered in a pool of hot dal, howling in pain. She leapt towards Ranju and hauled her off the floor into her arms. Ranju had accidentally knocked over the dal.

After washing her feet with cold water and calming her down, Mamta thought: Oh my God, how can I be so irresponsible? I need to get a grip on my life. This is not what Ram would have respected. She decided to reclaim her life and move forward, however difficult it may be for her. It had been two months since Ram had died. Mamta decided to resume work and Ranju was back to being with Gita aunty.

Mrs Sareen allowed Ranju to accompany her mother to work. She also offered to pay Mamta's rent because she didn't want to lose her favourite employee. Gita continued to look after Ranju in the evenings and steadfastly refused to accept any money in return. At work, Mamta ensured that Ranju never entered Mrs Sareen's house. She feared that Ranju would distract her while working, or break some expensive artifact. She did not even allow her daughter to use the swing in the garden. So each morning Ranju would wait for her mother in the guard's cabin.

The monsoons went on longer than usual, and the mosquitoes were in no mood to spare the little girl. By the end of the morning she would have angry red lumps on her arms and legs but Mamta, engulfed in sorrow, would not even notice. Eventually the guard, who had grown fond of Ranju, bought a tube of mosquito repellent. He would rub it on her arms and legs. As the days slipped by and winter approached, he mustered his courage and asked Mrs Sareen for a heater, who readily agreed.

Every morning, while her mother was busy inside the house, Ranju would tug at the guard's hand, pointing towards the swings. He would give in to her demand every once in a while when Mrs Sareen was not home. But his apprehension was not lost on the girl. She refused to go inside the house even when Mrs Sareen invited her to her children's birthday parties. Eventually, Ranju grew to resent their swanky cars, their expensive clothes and the fuss her mother made over them. Mrs Sareen would often ask Mamta why Ranju was so distant and aloof. She concluded that the girl was shy and had not adjusted to the loss of her father.

With Ram's income no longer coming in, Mamta found she was unable to manage on her earnings from Mrs Sareen and was forced to take up a second job at the riding school behind her slum. This job required her to come in at 5:30 every morning before the school opened at six. All Mamta had to do was prepare tea for the owner, Mrs Verma, clean the office and help the children put on their helmets. She would just lock the door from outside and leave Ranju sleeping. The slum was safe enough and there was no point in taking her along. Mamta would rush back home at 7:30, wake Ranju up, give her breakfast and take her along to Mrs Sareen's.

After a year, Mamta adjusted to her new routine and her solitude. She missed her family but the thought of going back to the village and becoming a burden to her brother drove her to work harder. Ranju started going to a goverment school and loved her new environment. At least she was now spared the need to go to Mrs Sareen's house. She missed the guard, whom she had begun to call chachu, but was relieved not to have to inhale the smoke of his beedis. She had hated the cold winter in his cabin and the mosquito-filled monsoon before it.

At four years old, Ranju's resemblance to her father grew more marked. She was tall for her age and had her father's chiselled jawline, broad forehead and friendly demeanour. Her shoulder-length curly locks framed an oval face. Her eyes had a mischievous twinkle like her mother.

At school she felt at home. Almost all the children walked back home with their mothers and few rode on their father's bicycles. Her best friend, Pinky, also lived in DID Colony. They would hold hands as they walked home after school, chirping like little sparrows as they trailed behind their mothers. Ranju missed having a sibling and often invited Pinky home. Sundays became their special day when Pinky's mother invited Ranju over. She loved playing hopscotch and enjoyed the Coke she was offered. Pinky was like her, her home was similar to hers. There was no place in it for Mamta and Pinky's mother, Sita, to sit and drink a cup of tea peacefully. They were all part of her world. However, their joys were incomparable to Mrs Sareen's children, she felt. There was a stark difference between them.

With the little money she managed to save Mamta would indulge Ranju twice a year, at Holi and Diwali, by taking her shopping to Sarojni Nagar Market. On these occasions Mamta would buy her new clothes and her favourite rasmalai. Although Ranju enjoyed Holi and the mischief of throwing colour on passersby, it came a distant second to Diwali. For Ranju, Diwali was magic. She would help her mother fix a string of fairy lights at the entrance of their hut, and wait impatiently for the moment when night fell. The year after her father's passing, her mother pulled out a packet of phuljaris from under her pillow to surprise her. Every year, Mamta also brought home bundle of hand-me-downs from Mrs Sareen's children.

'Why do you force me to wear clothes given by Sareen aunty? I want my own dresses, Ma,' she would sneer. Mamta would let it pass.

The bustle of Sarojini Nagar Market fascinated Ranju. She enjoyed the jam-packed bus ride to the market and seldom fussed about what she wanted to buy. On her birthday Mamta would allow her to choose a dress, clips, six plastic bangles and a pair of sandals. She and Pinky would later sit with her new posessions and discuss them for days.

Mamta loved Ranju and went out her way to make her happy. It was her way of holding on to Ram, after months of depression and neglect. Her unswerving desire was to educate Ranju, and fulfill their dream for her to acquire a skill like her father, and never be compelled to work as a servant in a household, like her mother.

3

One early spring morning, Mrs Sareen's garden, dazzling with different coloured flowers, looked splendid. Mamta was absorbed in cleaning the window panes in Mrs Sareen's bedroom when she looked out of the window and noticed an unfamiliar face in the garden. Mrs Sareen had retired the old gardener.

This must be the new fellow, she thought to herself. She returned to making the beds, but found herself frequently looking out of the window. The new gardener was tall, like Ram. As he bent over to clip the hedge his long straight hair fell over his eyes, forcing him to sweep it back every other minute. He looked fetching with his large eyes and bronze skin, and his sharp pointed nose had a hint of arrogance.

Unconsciously, she found herself staring at him till Mrs Sareen called out for a glass of water. Mamta had not been aware of another man since Ram's death. Abashed by her sudden interest she immediately turned away. He didn't look like a Bihari, and she concluded that he was probably from West Bengal. What surprised Mamta was his striped shirt, jeans and sneakers. It was his first day at work and his uniform was yet to be ordered. Mrs Sareen liked her staff to be immaculately dressed.

He was watering the plants with great care, bending every now and then to remove a dry leaf from the flower beds and throwing it into a plastic bag. He was also plucking fresh flowers for Mrs Sareen's morning puja. Mamta could not get herself away from the window. He drew closer and noticing her, he smiled. Surprising herself, Mamta smiled back.

Later that morning when she was on her way home, she met him at the gate and gathered the courage to talk to him.

'Are you the new gardener?'

'Yes, I've just moved from Bengal and have rented a shanty in DID Colony.'

'Oh! I live there too with my daughter,' said Mamta. Her radiant smile shocked the guard, for since Ram's death he had not seen her greet her colleagues with a smile.

'You will like the Sareens very much,' Mamta continued, effusively. 'I have been working with them for years. By the way, my name is Mamta.'

'I'm Ganesh, it's good to hear that we are neighbours,' he replied, with a broad smile. 'Maybe we can walk to work together every morning, if your husband doesn't mind.'

'I'm a widow,' Mamta's face fell as she whispered in a low tone and walked away. But at the corner she turned around to look at him. He had raised his hand to wave goodbye. She smiled and waved back at him.

Ganesh stayed on her mind till she reached Ranju's school. Walking home, she found herself paying little attention to her daughter's account of the day. A pang of guilt shot through her. Was this all it took to fill up the gap that Ram had left in her heart?

Mamta dropped Ranju to school early the next morning and her eagerness to see Ganesh was almost palpable. Walking towards Mrs Sareen's bungalow, she saw him standing at the top of the road, smoking a cigarette. Ganesh moved towards her and greeted her.

'Can we hurry?' he asked directly with a smile. 'I have been waiting for you and I'm already ten minutes late. I don't want to be reprimanded on my second day at work.'

Mamta smiled back, flattered. 'It's good of you to have stayed back,' she said softly, looking straight into his eyes.

Ganesh was staring at her too, before she quickly looked away.

'I believe you come to work in the evening as well,' Ganesh asked. 'What time do you finish?'

'At six,' she replied and couldn't help adding, 'It will be nice to have company on my way home.' But fearing the unspoken questions she would see in Gita's eyes, she hurriedly added, 'My friend and daughter wait for me at the top of the road every day.' Then another thought struck her, 'But the previous gardener would finish work at five. Has memsaab asked you to work an hour longer?'

'No, she hasn't. I thought I'd wait for you. But you can carry on with your daughter and I'll see you tomorrow,' replied Ganesh, with a hint of disappointment.

'I come in an hour early sometimes, so we can leave at five together. It will be nice to give Ranju a surprise once in a while,' Mamta said spontaneously. She regretted her utterance as soon as the words left her mouth. But it was too late. Ganesh looked at her and gave her a broad grin.

When Mamta and Ganesh walked into Mrs Sareen's gate together, ten minutes later, the guard gawked at them. Ganesh said a polite hello while Mamta avoided his eyes and walked into the house.

Mamta's excitement lingered all day. She was restless when she went home in the afternoon and hovered around the windows when she was at work later that evening, trying to catch a glimpse of him. She knew she was falling in love and that her neighbours would mock her and accuse her of having forgotten Ram too soon. She had the right to choose her path and stand up for herself. Times had changed and widows were remarrying. Was it really so sinful to desire a man again? No, she told herself. Fate had brought Ganesh to Mrs Sareen's door and nobody would stop her from following its dictates

The afternoon shift felt like the longest two hours of her life. She decided to stop at the chaiwala on her way home and spend some time with Ganesh alone. She knew private time with him wasn't something she would be rewarded with often.

Ganesh was waiting for her with his bicycle when she walked out of Mrs Sareen's gate. He offered her a ride but she preferred to walk.

'Do you want to stop for tea and samosas?' Mamta hesitantly asked Ganesh. 'I would have invited you home, but the neighbours will unnecessarily dream up stories.'

The camaraderie and comfort between them was spontaneous and evident. Over chai, Mamta poured her heart to him, telling him how she had lost Ram and how she had struggled afterwards. Ganesh felt empathy, but was relieved that she didn't have a husband. Gita and Ranju were sitting under the neem tree when they saw Mamta come around the bend with Ganesh. Ranju ran to her mother and flung her arms around her.

'I thought I would surprise you with a samosa, my princess,' Mamta said hugging her. As she introduced them to Ganesh, Ranju hid behind her mother tugging at her sari. Gita was cold and wary. Sensing her hostility, Ganesh offered to take Ranju for an ice-cream around the corner. Ranju looked at her mother for permission and Mamta nodded.

Gita was surprised by Mamta's unusual behaviour. She appreciated how attentive Mamta had always been with Ranju but she stared at her with raised eyebrows.

'He's my employer's new gardener and lives in our basti,' she tried to placate Gita.

As the two friends walked a few steps in silence, Mamta sensed Gita was upset and knew her friend felt possessive towards her. She would not be open to a new man in her life. She had stood by Mamta through her tragedy and felt she owned her.

'Be careful, Mamta! These men can take advantage of you. I didn't like the way he looked at you. Besides, how can you send your daughter away with a stranger?'

'Don't worry,' replied Mamta. 'He's a nice person... there's something about him which gives me a good feeling.' Gita was silent but frowned in disbelief as they approached Gita's hut.

Ganesh brought Ranju back half an hour later. 'Ma! I went and ate golgappas and ice-cream with uncle...and he gave me ride on his cycle!' Ranju squealed in delight. Mamta was touched.

On a strange impulse, Mamta asked Ganesh to stay and eat with them. It was only his second day in the slum, she would tell Gita later. Ganesh was carrying a small bag full of vegetables that he had bought while waiting for Mamta. With a flourish he offered it to her.

'This is for you,' he said with a smile. 'Perhaps, once in a while you can cook for me as well.' Mamta shyly took the vegetables from him and nodded.

As the days passed, this became their routine. Ganesh would bring some vegetables every other evening, and Mamta would cook while Ganesh helped Ranju with her homework. A bond began to grow between Ranju and her favourite uncle. Every Sunday, he would take her to the zoo or India Gate for an ice-cream treat. Ranju loved watching the gas balloons fly into the sky and the bicycle ride back home.

Mamta would accompany them on every alternate

Sunday, when she had her day off. Meanwhile Gita strongly objected to their intimacy and never missed a chance to tell Mamta off. She had helped Mamta through her desolation after Ram's death and felt deeply protective towards her. But as the months went by Ganesh slowly replaced Ram in both Mamta and Ranju's life.

4

Mamta and Ganesh carried on their romance without bothering about the world. Every night, they would spend a couple of hours together when Ranju fell asleep. They enjoyed being alone and had little to squabble about, except when Mamta talked about marriage.

'We can't carry on like this,' she would complain every other month. She resented Gita's constant hostility towards Ganesh. Moreover, she was apprehensive about how Ranju would react to their relationship, once she was old enough to understand. Mamta loved Ganesh to death and wanted permanency. She craved to have a normal life and, above all, she wanted the slum-dwellers to respect her relationship. Ranju would be more than happy to have him as her father. A happily-ever-after was all she truly wished for.

'I cannot marry you, Mamta. My family will never accept you and they will disown me. I have to adhere to their wishes and marry within my community. I'm the only child of my parents and can't let them down. Besides you are three years my senior and a widow with a child. My parents will never accept our relationship. I love you, but I will never lie or mislead you into something I can't do.'

The truth hurt her but all she did was slump in a corner. Life without Ganesh seemed preposterous. She was resigned to live one day at a time, just hoping for the best. One evening, Mamta found Ganesh unusually quiet and distracted.

'What's the matter, Ganesh? Is something bothering you?'

Unable to hold back he immediately blurted out, 'I've just received a letter from my father and they have fixed my marriage for next month. I will have to return to the village in four days.'

Mamta was stunned. The roti on the tawa started to burn. Ganesh stood up from the bed and sat down on the floor beside her. He put the tawa aside on a folded newspaper. Snuggling up to Mamta, he gave her a tight hug.

'It is not easy for me either,' he whispered into her ear. 'Please, don't make this worse, Mamta. We knew this would happen one day… I promise I will leave my wife in the village and come back to you. It's something I just have to do to please my parents.'

Mamta did not say a word. She pushed him back and stared at his face as her eyes welled up. As they fell down her blouse in big drops, she did not wipe them off. Why hide her sorrow? She knew in that moment that Ganesh would never be hers alone. She was alone again.

Her copious tears melted Ganesh's heart, but his hands were tied. He pulled her closer. 'You are like a candle which illuminates my life and I'm like the wind that is blowing it out,' he said. Mamta sat mute; quarrelling or complaining was futile.

That night, they made love. Then Mamta gave him dinner and curled up in bed, crying herself to sleep. After that night, she did not speak or spend time with Ganesh, and he left for his village four days later.

'Don't worry, Mamta. I will be back and I won't let you down. There are things in life that I have to do to keep the peace and please my elders. But you will always remain a part of my life,' he assured her before leaving.

Ranju was sad too, and she caught his hand and walked him to the auto. Ganesh waved at the two fragile figures standing under the neem tree till he completely lost sight of them.

'When will Ganesh return?' Gita probed Mamta, with a hint of sarcasm in her voice.

'He's gone to visit his parents in the village, as his father has been ill lately.' Mamta wasn't going to confide in her friend. She did not want Gita or the others taunting her. She had to trust Ganesh and hope he kept his promise.

Ganesh regularly called her from the village, reassuring her that he meant every word he had promised her. She accepted her destiny, kept their secret close to her chest and carried on with her life, waiting for him to return. But living alone was daunting and expensive for Mamta. Ganesh had helped out with the groceries and looked after Ranju when Mamta had to help at Mrs Sareen's dinner parties. The extra money was a blessing which helped her give Ranju a banana and a glass of milk everyday and pomegranate twice a week.

At nights the darkness scared her, and she walked across to Ganesh's hut to lie on his bed, drawing comfort in his smell. He had left the keys with her, to reassure her that he was coming back. With each passing day Mamta grew adamant about persuading him to live with her. She could not be alone again. Ganesh had promised never to bring his wife back to Delhi. This mere thought brought a smile to her face. Her excitement of living like a married couple became the core of her existence.

The following month, Ganesh was back in Delhi after his marriage, just as he had promised. However, he made it clear that his father would be visiting soon and he did not want her to be a concubine. Nor did he want them living together. Mamta was devastated and argued herself hoarse. But she gave up eventually, despondent and jealous. When Ganesh was around, she spoke only when spoken to, never initiating any conversation.

Ranju, on the other hand, was happy to see Ganesh uncle. She relished the sandesh and cuddled the rag doll which he had brought back for her from his village. For the first week after his return, Ganesh took Ranju for an ice-cream treat every day, and made an extra effort in placating Mamta. However, he soon got tired of her tantrums and resentment. One night, after Ranju was asleep, Ganesh tried holding Mamta in his arms, but she wriggled out saying she wasn't in the mood.

'How long are you going to behave like this, Mamta?' Ganesh retorted with anger. 'If you don't want to be with me, you should have told me so when I called you several times from the village. I would have brought my wife back with me.'

Mamta whirled around while combing her hair, flabbergasted. She stood still for a moment and then ran into his arms sheepishly.

'I feel jealous, Ganesh, and I can't help it,' she said, blinking back a solitary tear. Wrapping his arms around her, Ganesh kissed her and playfully threw her on the bed.

'Don't be ridiculous, Mamta! You are the love of my life,' he smiled. Their little world was filled with sunshine once again and life was back to as it had been.

Ranju would often ask Ganesh to come to school after work. 'Meet my Papa,' she would proudly say, holding his hand, as she introduced him to her friends. Ranju had accepted him as her father and if this is what made her happy, he could go along. The family ate dinner together every night, after which Ganesh would leave their hut for his night cigarette and Mamta would put Ranju to sleep and spend time with Ganesh in his hut thereafter.

A few months later, as they sat down for dinner, Mamta announced, 'I'm pregnant, Ganesh and I'm going to keep the baby.'

Ganesh continued eating his dal-roti, his expression stoic. A few minutes later, Mamta turned off the stove and came around to sit next to him. Placing her head on his shoulders, she said, 'I love you enough to keep this baby, knowing very well that you will never marry me. I have a small request. Can we just live together and tell everyone in the slum that we are married?'

Ganesh didn't say anything. Abruptly standing up, he washed his hands and walked straight out of her shanty.

Mamta ran after him but he firmly shut the door of his hut. She placed both her hands on the door and pressed her face as close as possible, so no one could hear her cries.

'Why are you quiet, Ganesh? Say something please. Your silence is killing me.'

Opening his door slightly, he said, 'Are you trying to blackmail me? I strongly disapprove of having a baby outside wedlock. I want to father a child proudly and not in this manner. I cannot marry you and I'm not willing to have a child and complicate our lives further.'

Leaving the door open, Ganesh lay down on his bed. Mamta followed him and slid under the covers. She was going to coax him into the throngs of passion and get him to agree to live with her. But Ganesh stood his ground despite her threats to break up with him and continue with her pregnancy.

'The choice is yours, Mamta. If you defy me and do as you please, you will force me to leave you and go back to my village against my will.'

Giving his final word, Ganesh turned his back to her and lay motionless. Mamta didn't remove her arm from around him, clinging and trying to reinforce her desires between her sobs. Ganesh remained unmoved. He knew that capitulating to Mamta would mean giving up his wife and eventually, his parents. This was something he was not willing to do.

The next morning, Mamta and Ganesh went about

their business, without exchanging a single word or glance. A week passed by and Mamta was also adamant. She wanted to have the baby at any cost. Her resolve made Ganesh angrier with every passing day. He would leave the vegetables by her door, never entering her house. If Mamta didn't abort their baby, he would be forced to return to the village and break all ties with her. Mamta wanted the baby, but didn't want to lose Ganesh. Ranju, confused by the goings on, asked her mother more than once, 'Why doesn't uncle eat dinner with us anymore? Is he angry with us, Ma?'

Fed up with her constant questioning and Ganesh's apathy, Mamta would leave the room without an answer. She would sit under the neem tree and think of how to convince Ganesh. Gita would often join her and carry on about her own day till Mamta politely excused herself and went back home.

When Ranju visited Ganesh in his shanty, he would call her in, sit her on his lap and look at her with teary eyes. He didn't want to lose them, but if he conceded to Mamta's wish, he would be compelled to run parallel families: something he did not want. And then one day his secret would stare him in the face and the villagers would taunt his father and shame him. He knew he was being ignoble and selfish, but he was convinced he was doing the right thing. He was a fair man, but when it came to Mamta he had to sacrifice his beliefs completely. He was emotionally weak and ignored his hypocrisy.

'I have to go back to the village and I'm sad leaving

you behind,' Ganesh told Ranju impulsively one evening when she came visiting him. Inadvertently, Ranju went running back to her shanty and blurted to her mother, 'Uncle is leaving us and going back to his village. Why is he upset with us? I'm a good girl and I do whatever he asks me to. I also colour a picture for him every day and did a drawing of him and me just yesterday. Ma, why don't you go to his room and convince him to stay?'

Mamta was lying down with the pillow over her face as the sheer emotional turmoil of the past two weeks had drained all her energy. The yellow light from the bulb looked like a ball of fire ready to swallow her. Ranju's voice pierced into her ears like the cacophony of a wedding band. She sprang up from her bed, and ran towards the door. She knew she had to give in to Ganesh if she wanted him to stay. Charging towards the door, she fell on the aluminium bucket of water lying in the middle of the hut, on her stomach. The sudden, forceful impact bent the rim of the bucket and Mamta slipped off and lay sprawled on the wet floor. She reached out for the door to help her stand up again. She was determined to reach Ganesh's shanty. Ranju was too shocked to say or do anything. Mamta reached Ganesh's hut and flopped on to the ground, wailing hysterically. Ganesh stood there looking at Mamta, unsure of what had happened. Ranju had followed her mother, and stood there, terrified.

'Ma fell down,' said Ranju in a meek voice when Mamta fainted.

'Ranju, go bring Gita aunty right away!' was

all Ganesh could say. 'Wait, wait! Let me see what's happened.' Confiding in Gita meant inviting gossip and slander from the entire slum. Telling all and sundry she was pregnant and he was married would make things worse. Mamta gained consciousness just as Ganesh was putting on his shoes to carry her to a nearby hospital.

'I'm okay now. Just give me a glass of water,' Mamta said, feeling a bit woozy. Ganesh lifted her off the floor and put her on the bed. She clung to him, sobbing. Ranju ran to her mother and held her hand. With the situation under control, Ganesh put Ranju on the second mattress in his room and slept with Mamta in his arms. He cried like a child all night, feeling guilty about how much anguish he was causing the woman he loved. She clung to him too, with no intentions of letting go. Where was the solution to their problem? Each wanted the other to cave in.

5

The next morning, Mamta woke up tired and weary. The day's endless tasks seemed extremely daunting. However, she had to go to work, she wasn't privileged enough to spend the day resting. Mrs Verma would be waiting for her morning cup of tea, she had to get Ranju ready for school, prepare her tiffin and be at Mrs Sareen's by 8:30. Mamta dragged herself out of bed, reaching for the biscuits and Britannia cake which she would carry back to her shanty for Ranju's mid-day meal. She had no energy to make her favourite cucumber chutney sandwiches. Ganesh tossed and turned in bed but continued sleeping.

Suddenly, she sensed a warm liquid running down her left thigh. Unwittingly wiping it with her salwar, she continued pondering over the unpleasantness of the previous evening. There was a discomfort in her lower abdomen, which she ignored. She poured herself a glass of water and bent over to pick up Ranju from the floor and carry her back to her hut. But again, the pain and watery substance between her thighs compelled her to pull down her salwar to see what was bothering her. A blackish liquid trickling towards her knees immediately confirmed that her baby was in danger. She instantly ran outside, towards the common toilet at the far end of the slum, leaving behind a trail of blood. Gita was walking ten metres behind her in a daze, too sleepy to notice anything. There was already a short queue outside and Mamta restlessly waited for her turn. When she reached the toilet she knew at once she had lost her baby. Walking out, she broke down on Gita's shoulder.

'What has happened?' Gita asked, concerned. Mamta slid down and crouched on the floor.

With one hand she held on to Gita and with the other she covered her face and said without thinking, 'I've lost my baby. I was two months pregnant.'

Gita stared at her stupefied. 'Pregnant?' she repeated. Immediately Mamta realized what she had said, but it was too late. Everyone in the colony knew she had lost her baby before Ganesh woke up that morning.

Ganesh sat beside Mamta in the hospital relieved, not yet knowing how to react. He glanced at her, lying on the bed, vacantly staring at the ceiling. Gita held back her anger and sat silently outside the room. As the nurse came in and gave them a discharge slip, Mamta slid her feet off the bed and sat with her legs dangling for a few seconds. She then abruptly stood up, wore her slippers and walked out of the room without a second look at Ganesh. Destiny had been cruel and Ganesh had finally got what he wanted.

Mamta had lost a very precious part of herself, a part

of Ganesh, which she adored even before it was born. Why was her destiny crippled? Why did she have to lose what she loved and wanted most? Her breath felt heavy and her heart felt like it was going to come to a grinding halt.

Gita looked at Ganesh with contempt. She failed to understand why Mamta was so absorbed in a relationship with a man for whom she was a mere vessel. However, right now Mamta needed empathy and any other discussion would have to wait for a later time. Mamta sank into her bed when she got home. The last two weeks had taken its toll physically, mentally and emotionally.

Ganesh followed her back to her room quietly, without saying a word. Just being around in any which way, to attend to her, was important for him. Mamta's distress did bring tears to his eyes every now and then. Being callous and selfish was never his intention. It took Mamta many weeks to accept her loss but she had to put this unfortunate incident behind her and move forward.

'Why don't you marry Ganesh?' Gita asked Mamta a few days later.

'We will, once he convinces his parents. They won't easily accept me. I'm not from their caste and I'm a widow with a child,' Mamta said without hesitation. She was never going to reveal her lover's marital status. Gita kept on pressing her every week.

'I care for you and I think you should open your eyes to the truth. This man will never marry you,' she said, unable to contain herself.

Gita's concern for Mamta was apparent, but what

could she tell her friend? That she was weak and unable to live without Ganesh? She cared very deeply for him and liked him being a good father to her daughter. He helped with the expenses and above all, he loved them both immensely. If she wanted to be part of his life she had to accept her situation. Gita would never understand, she knew that. No one would.

'People in the colony criticise you all the time and I can't stop anyone. I dislike it,' Gita said but Mamta turned a deaf ear.

All the women in the slum looked at Mamta with contempt, gossipped about her and thought she was an ignoble woman. They stopped talking to her and never missed a chance to hit her below the belt. Mamta soon became a pariah. All she cared about was having Ganesh by her side. He offered for them to move away to another slum a few kilometres away, but Mamta was adamant about being close to her current employers. Gita slowly turned hostile when she realized Mamta was too stubborn. Jagdish asked Gita to stop hanging around Mamta, saying she was a bad influence but continued to keep an eye on Ranju—they owed it to Ram.

After a couple of months, it was time for Ganesh to go back to the village on his annual leave. Despite her efforts to stay calm, Mamta was panicking. She'd return to her room at nights weeping, and crouched on her bed unsure of what the future had in store. She'd toss the pillow across the room and then cuddle another, her gaze settling on the door, wanting to run across to Ganesh's hut and ask him not to go back. Ganesh could sense her anxiety and promised her that nothing would change. He assured her he would be back in a month, promising to call her as often as he could. He now had a wife and phoning Mamta every day would not be easy. Conscious that she didn't have the power to change anything, Mamta was resigned to her destiny and accepted everything in silence.

6

Ganesh's wife, Parvati, was a petite girl, seven years younger than him. She was fair-skinned and her long hair flowed down to her waist. Her high cheek bones and almond-like eyes, small nose and full lips drew a pretty picture. She was shy, soft spoken and reserved, but it did not matter to Ganesh. He accepted her as his parent's choice. She had lived with them since their marriage and never neglected or disobeyed them. She secretly loved her husband and longed to be with him, but could never dare to express her fervour, as it would be considered inappropriate.

Ganesh was restrained around her and barely spoke to her even on the phone. She hadn't had enough time with him after their wedding. She longed to be wrapped in his arms and kiss him all night. She dreamt of living a life with him in the city. She was eager to start a family. She waited patiently for a full year and now, at last, she could not wait to be reunited with her darling Ganesh. Her in-laws adored her and appreciated her company. But they were growing old and cooking and looking after them was becoming dreary for Parvati.

Once a week, Parvati covered her head and demurely walked beside her father-in-law for a mile to the nearest telephone booth, just to hear Ganesh's voice. There wasn't much she could say with his father standing next to her. Ganesh knew he neglected Parvati and felt guilty at times, trying hard to draw himself away from Mamta. But he couldn't help himself. His passion and love was solely for Mamta.

The day he was to come, Parvati had cooked all day, wanting to hear a few words of praise from Ganesh. Kosho Mangsho, narkol chollar dal, shukto and mishti doi, all Ganesh's favourite dishes, were on the menu. It was months since he had eaten an authentic Bengali meal. Ganesh's mother looked at Parvati adoringly. How blessed her son was to have her as his wife.

Their modest home had two rooms on the ground floor, with a kitchen and a toilet, and one large room on the first floor. The wrought iron staircase leading to the first floor was steep and shaky, with a few missing steps. Parvati slept upstairs.

The one-mile journey from the village market, where the bus had dropped off Ganesh, was arduous. It was a narrow lane, with dense shrubs along the edge. It was a pain to cycle along the shrubs without jumping off to regain balance. The stray dogs in the vicinity were an added nuisance. Their population had grown since the last time Ganesh visited his village. The dogs were aggressive and biting at the heels of passersby and darting into the shrubs for rats and rabbits. As the narrow lane merged onto the wider main road leading to the local post office, Ganesh glanced around at the men, women and children moving around aimlessly or sitting in small groups, talking. Life in the village was so different and laidback from the chaos and hustle-bustle of the city. The villagers were content with their tranquil existence. Life was hard and the income negligible, but there was a peace.

Reaching his home, Ganesh saw Parvati standing on the veranda talking with a friend. She had waited a full year for him to come home without grumbling. She had served his parents selflessly. He felt guilt and revulsion for not being able to love his wife. He had to make it up to her in different ways...but how? He blinked and looked away, directing his gaze towards his mother who sat on the steps leading up to the house. Parvati saw him the minute he took the turn into their lane and hurried inside to inform her father-in-law. His parents were at the door to welcome him. Ganesh ran the last few metres to hug them. His eyes welled up with tears as his father embraced him with trembling hands.

'Welcome home, my son! We are so happy to see you,' said his father as his voice quivered.

'We have been counting the days,' Ganesh's mother kissed his forehead. Parvati just stood in the corner and stared at the family reunion. 'He must be really hungry. Give him some bananas and put the rice to boil,' his mother ordered Parvati in a tone of authority.

Ganesh ate his meal without saying a word about the food. He sat with his father, expressing concern over his health, and was relieved to know their land was finally yielding results. It had been a good year and the potato crop had sold well.

'I was thinking of planting some fruit trees,' said his father. 'There was an expert scientist who came to our village last month and advised us to try different kinds of farming.' Ganesh's opinion and consent was important to him.

'You already have a lot on your plate, Baba. How can you do all this alone?' said Ganesh, trying to dissuade his father. His ailing health bothered him. 'You don't need to take on any additional workload.'

'I want you to come back to the village and look after your land. We need you here. How long can you leave Parvati here with us?' The anguish and infirmity of old age were palpable in his voice.

However, Ganesh had no plans of living in the village and deserting Mamta. He joked with his father and said, 'You are still young, and can manage the farm for a long time. Don't worry, I'm with you for a month to sort out anything that needs attention.' He hugged his father every now and then to assure him things would be fine.

'I'll give you a back massage tomorrow with some mustard oil boiled with garlic. Don't worry so much, you are still healthy.'

At the end of the day Parvati went upstairs to her room and paced the verandah impatiently. What was so important for Ganesh to discuss with his father that couldn't wait for another day? Ganesh sat on the floor next to his father's bed, talking to his parents for hours till his mother eventually asked him to go upstairs and sleep.

With an apparent reluctance, Ganesh climbed the stairs. He didn't want to make love to Parvati, but knew that he had to do what was expected of him. There was nothing he could do to escape it. Parvati, on the other hand, was gradually losing patience and aching to be with her Ganesh. She slipped into a new nightdress which she had hidden in the far corner of her cupboard and left her thick mane open. As she heard him climb the stairs, Parvati ran to the door and stood there waiting for him to enter the room, her pulse fluttering. She looked at him from under her lashes, wanting to run into his arms and embrace him. But she took a step back when he just walked past her into the washroom, without even a glance in her direction. Parvati swallowed hard and quietly went to the bed, sitting on the edge, waiting for him to emerge.

Ganesh had a quick shower, changed into a fresh t-shirt and walked out knowing what was expected. He sat next to her on the bed and reached out to hold her hand. Once he fulfilled his duty he stretched out on the bed staring at the fan listlessly. He was tired and had to wake up early morning to go with his father for a walk through the fields. Parvati was happy just resting her head on his arm, glad that he was finally home. As Ganesh stared into the darkness he could hear Parvati breathing in his ear; it felt a bit ticklish. He looked at her and turned his face away, his thoughts drifting to Mamta.

The next morning, Ganesh was up early. He jumped

out of bed and immediately went downstairs to drink his morning tea with his parents. The earlier he went to survey the crop the more he would save himself from the scorching heat.

'I don't think you should come to the fields today, as you seem a little tired,' Ganesh told his father.

'No, I'm fine. Let's go. I want to show you the new crop in Shyam's farm which I want to plant next season,' his father replied.

Walking towards his fields, Ganesh was soaking in the tranquillity and the exhilarating smell of the soil. Suddenly, his father collapse to the ground. He had lost consciousness. The only person around was his neighbour Raja, standing at a distance and feeding his cows. Ganesh shouted across the field, asking for help. Raja came running in a flash, holding a mug of water in his hand. The heat had probably drained his father's energy. Ganesh and Raja picked the old man up and carried him home. Ganesh's mother panicked when she saw her husband unconscious and kept tugging at Ganesh's sleeve, while Parvati patiently tried to console her.

'Go bring a doctor, Raja! He doesn't seem to be okay,' Ganesh said. Raja ran out of their house at once. Then, suddenly his father touched his finger and opened his eyes, but he was unable to move. His body was limp and cold. He was helpless and couldn't swallow any water. The family was terrified. His wife sat on the bed next to him, rubbing his hand and urging him to keep his eyes open.

Parvati held her mother-in-law and consoled her with

words of reassurance. 'Come and sit on the chair, Ma. Raja will be here with the doctor in ten minutes,' she said.

Dumbstruck and frightened, Ganesh sat on the bed next to his father. Minutes later, the doctor arrived and suspected paralysis. It seemed that his father's left side had been badly affected.

'Take him to the hospital immediately. They will take good care of him,' the doctor suggested. The family stood in shock, as Ganesh's mother sank on the floor crying. Parvati sat next to her trying to calm her down, and Ganesh and Raja immediately ran out of the house to make arrangements to rush him to the hospital. Ganesh's father had to be carried in a collapsible bed till the bus stop, after which he was taken to the hospital in a taxi. Ganesh loved his father more than anyone else and he knew his world would crumble to pieces if anything happened to him.

They spent two weeks in the hospital, after which Ganesh brought his father home. There was substantial improvement in his condition, but his lower left side was immobile. It was certain that he would never plough his field again. All responsibilities of the household now fell on Ganesh. Caught up in his father's medical problems, he hadn't called Mamta for over three weeks. He was afraid he would deliberate, ruminate, rationalize and talk himself into going back if he called her. He visited the hospital during the day, sat with his father, helped him with his exercises and fed him before returning home. At night he would sit with his mother in his arms, consoling her and keeping her hopes alive.

But what had he done for Parvati except take her for granted? She had been supportive and emotionally strong during this crisis. She had taken complete charge of the family and hadn't said a word to Ganesh. He would come into their bedroom exhausted, too tired to even talk to her. She looked after the fields, fed the cows, cooked and cleaned for the family and constantly looked after her mother-in-law. Ganesh eventually began to appreciate Parvati's selflessness through all his hardships—but couldn't fall in love with her. His affection for Mamta was irreplaceable. Every time he thought of her smiling face, the urge to be with her overpowered him. He felt trapped by his circumstances and responsibilities. Ganesh urged Parvati to train a young village boy who could help her plough the fields. He had to return to his dear Mamta and Delhi. He was unable to deny this uneasy truth.

7

Thousands of miles away from him, Mamta sat outside with her head against her door, looking at the sky. She was unable to curb the tears flowing from her eyes. She couldn't help but blame her destiny.

Why did Ram leave me alone? she asked herself. The emotional void and insecurity scared her. But this is what she had signed up for. She knew it was time to take a decision, and it was in her hands to keep worrying or to finally get a grip on her life. She wanted to walk across to Gita's shanty and pour her heart out but she knew she couldn't do that. She went back to bed and laid next to Ranju, trying hard to fall asleep.

It had been a month and Mamta hadn't heard from Ganesh. Anguished and unsure, she would often snap at Ranju during the day, only to regret it later. Ranju's constant queries about her favourite uncle soon died down. She didn't want to be scolded at the very mention of his name. She slowly began to resent Ganesh and felt he was the cause of their misery. Meanwhile Mamta's troubles surfaced even at her workplace. Mrs Sareen often asked her the reason behind her melancholy, even suggesting she take a week's leave.

'Everything is fine, memsaab,' Mamta would irritably respond.

She was too ashamed to share her distress with Mrs Sareen. There was only one solution to her misfortune—forget Ganesh. She was fed up with him, but couldn't push him away from her thoughts. How could he dare treat her so shabbily! She had agreed to every condition of his, but still his callousness knew no bounds. He had hurt her immensely. There was a deep feeling of humiliation, angst and defeat which she carried with her for weeks.

Mamta also had no answers to Gita's incessant probing into her life. She had believed that Ganesh loved her and would stand by her forever. She had trusted him blindly, but he had let her down. Like a beautiful dream, their relationship had come to an abrupt end. Mamta's judgement had deserted her completely.

Six months passed by and Mamta ultimately realized it was futile waiting for Ganesh, or his phone calls. She accepted she had been abandoned and had to fend for herself and Ranju. The slum-dwellers sniggered behind her back and kept her at arm's length. Their children weren't allowed to play with Ranju either. Gita, who had grudged Mamta's decision to be with Ganesh, was reluctant to overlook her indiscretions too. They were still friends but she was no longer Mamta's confidant.

Ranju had no one to play with when she got back from school. She felt like an outcaste. She would frequently go to the riding school and stand in the corner watching the children ride. She wished to be like them: ride in luxury cars, have a personal maid pour her a glass of juice or hand her a fruit after the class. Soon, she became acquainted with them. They often asked her to join them and offered her things to eat and drink. With time, she grew to like them and waved frantically to them when she saw them driving home. One little girl in particular, Shruti, shared her sandwiches and biscuits with her. She stayed back after class to talk to Ranju and encouraged her to learn English. She would bring picture books specially for her, and toiled hard to teach her English. Ranju longed to become an ace rider like Shruti, Mrs Verma's favourite student.

Dreaming a dream was one thing and realizing it was another. Mamta would turn a deaf ear to Ranju's desire of learning how to ride. It was painful refusing Ranju every time she asked for something. One night, after an argument, Ranju pushed her plate aside, stood up and strutted over to her mother who was warming the rotis.

She stood with her hands on her hips and defiantly asked her mother, 'Why can't I learn riding, Ma? I love the horses and I can also look after them for Verma aunty.'

'Don't indulge in unrealistic desires we can't afford, Ranju, as they will always leave you disappointed and unhappy.' Mamta glanced at her daughter with despair, as she stood with her downcast eyes.

But then all of a sudden, Ranju erupted, 'Why am I always deprived of everything? Uncle doesn't visit us anymore and we live in this horrible hut. I can neither learn riding, nor wear fancy clothes. I'm always wearing clothes given by your memsaab and I hate that.'

Mamta patiently held her daughter's hand and explained, 'Don't be envious of the luxuries enjoyed by others, my child. You have to study hard and achieve your goals. When you are grown up and go to a good college and get a good job, then you will have everything you desire. Unfortunately, your mother isn't educated and cannot give you all these things you want. But I won't make the same mistake with you. Have patience, you will get everything with time.'

'I'll help at the school and look after the horses, and then maybe I will be allowed riding too,' Ranju continued convincing her mother.

'Okay, I'll ask Mrs Verma,' Mamta said eventually.

It was futile trying to explain to Ranju that she was growing up in a different world and she could never enjoy luxuries such as riding lessons, unless she studied hard and carved her own destiny. Mamta pulled Ranju down besides her and hugged her. She fed her with her hands that night. They stayed up late watching television and eventually cuddled up together and went to sleep.

One evening, while sitting in the veranda, enjoying the cool breeze, Ganesh told his father, 'Baba, I need to get back to Delhi and my job as soon as possible. It's been so long and I haven't even informed my employer. We are not making enough money from the crops to sustain us. I have taught Tushar how to plough the fields. He will help Parvati while I am away and the extra money I make in Delhi will help us,' he fumbled, sensing his father growing impatience.

'If you want me to die, you are free to go back. I'm a sick man and my limbs don't work anymore. Your mother is old and your wife will give birth to a baby in six months. She can't go to the fields and work all day. You can kill all of us and then do what you want,' said his father indignantly.

Ganesh spent an hour trying to convince his parents and Parvati, but without much success. He grudgingly resigned to his fate and shut out any hopes of going back to Delhi. He hadn't called Mamta in all these months to give her any explanation. No amount of explaining would have helped Mamta calm down anyway. She would argue with him and the unpleasantness would only make it worse. Their sweet memories were what he chose to live with.

They both learnt to live without each other and carry on with their respective lives. Time helped them heal and slowly they faded out of each others' lives.

8

Another year passed and every day, Ganesh would spend long hours in the fields. He ate dinner with his parents, discussing the day's events and then his only child, Pralad, took over his evenings. He would spend time sitting with Pralad's school books and revelled in feeding him once in a while. They would often cycle to the village market to buy story books, stickers and colour pencils. Ganesh enjoyed reading stories to his son every night, often repeating his favourite ones, till he fell asleep in his arms. Pralad loved getting into bed with his father, resting his head on his arm and attentively watching him flip the pages and read to him. The illustrations fascinated him and he often stopped his father from turning the page. Once in a while, when Ganesh came home before dark he would play football with his son on the unpaved road outside their home and the neighbours' children often joined the fun.

Ganesh found infinite solace in these little moments. On Sundays, Pralad accompanied his father to the fields and frolicked around while Ganesh often ruminated about what his future would be. They had bought some additional land adjoining their farm and Ganesh was resigned to his fate of staying back home. Parvati often sensed indifference in her husband's attitude and was forced to demand her husband's time.

'We don't spend any time together and it's always about your work, parents or Pralad,' she would often complain.

It was challenging for Ganesh to give her a tiny place in his heart, but she surely deserved a bit of his time.

'I'll take you into town next week and buy you a nice sari. We can leave Pralad with Ma and Baba as they seldom get time with him alone.'

Parvati was happy he didn't go back to the city. She was easy to please her, and with a little pampering and care she was happy.

'I do need some new clothes,' she smiled and went up to her husband to plant a kiss on his cheek.

Ganesh appreciated her devotion to him and his family, but their relationship lacked intimacy. Parvati, in spite of her misgivings, eventually reconciled to their missing link. She loved Ganesh unconditionally and had tried hard to win his love. She questioned him several times but never got a satisfactory reply. They never fought or argued, and Parvati never gave him a reason to complain. She looked after his parents and their son with the utmost diligence. Their lives carried on without much ado.

Eight Years Later

The heavy monsoons that year devastated Ganesh's village. He lost everything: the crops and the house. The heavy rains had unleashed havoc in Khanakul, Hooghly District. The Mundeswari which flowed through the region carried water from the Damodar and joined the Ruparayan at the tri-junction of the Hooghly. The rivers had overflowed their banks and inundated the fields, destroying crops, causing loss of human life and cattle, and the destruction of property. The water had washed away everything that came in its way, submerging large areas of land and completely eroding the upper fertile soil. Many villages around the area had been engulfed by the flood waters and low-lying areas had turned into huge lakes. People had to be evacuated to higher and safer places, as the flood waters took over a month and a half to recede. Inadequate sanitation facilities and lack of government support led to greater health problems. Ganesh lost his father to malaria.

The destruction lingered for weeks after the debris were cleared. Ganesh and Parvati were unable to sleep, and Pralad often woke up at night clinging to his mother with fear. Ganesh's mother sat by the window just in case the floods attacked them again. They slept with a light on to comfort themselves, scared of what the darkness had in store.

The only positive outcome of the whole disaster was that it strengthened Parvati and Ganesh's relationship. Her ability to hold the family together touched a chord in his heart. He knew it would take him as long to heal emotionally as it would take him to rebuild his home. All that was left were the sweet memories of home.

But Ganesh had had no time to grieve. They had no food or water for a week and he had to find ways to transport basic essentials to his family. Their ground floor was submerged and animal carcasses floated outside their two-storeyed house. Ganesh had carried his father's body like a child in his arms for a mile to the cremation ground. It was the worst flood they had witnessed in their lifetime. It was intolerable for Ganesh to sit at home watching the water rise slowly, engulfing his whole life. He sobbed turbulently watching all his hard work being swept away one afternoon. After the water receded, everything was destroyed and they had no savings. A couple of months later, Ganesh returned to the city and try to rebuild their lives.

He entrusted Parvati with the responsibility of looking after his mother and Pralad, and promised to come home every three months. He was hesitant to leave them alone, but he had to find a way to support them. Parvati and Pralad accompanied him to the bus stop and bid him goodbye with dewy eyes. Ganesh stared at his wife and son after boarding the bus as they stood together painting a sorry picture. He knew his parents had chosen well for him and Parvati was a dream wife, but he still could not get himself to love her. He hated himself and wished he could give her a small part of his heart. But even after all these years, Mamta still had his heart.

9

Nothing had changed for Mamta, she had carried on working for Mrs Sareen and the riding school. Mrs Verma had very kindly allowed Ranju to join the school without paying any fee.

'Your mother tells me you want to learn riding,' Mrs Verma asked Ranju affectionately one day.

'Yes, aunty,' Ranju instantly replied. 'If you allow me to learn riding at the school, I promise to help you look after the horses.'

Mrs Verma chuckled at the little girl's enthusiasm.

'Oh my! You are still very young to work but we can strike a deal. Once you have learnt to ride, it will be your responsibility to work the horses which haven't been ridden on any particular day.'

Ranju broke into a smile, clinging to her mother's sari.

'Go touch aunty's feet and thank her like a good girl,' said her grateful mother.

Ranju ran to dive at Mrs Verma's feet but got a hug instead. She was ecstatic. This was her first point of entry into the world of the wealthy. In that moment, she made a firm resolve to study hard and carve a better life for herself and her mother.

Mamta carried on with her mundane existence as Ranju started going to the riding school with much enthusiasm. Occasionally, Ranju was also invited to birthday parties by her riding school peers. For such occasions, her mother had bought her a white lace dress with orange flowers on it. She also now owned a pair of black leather shoes and a white hair band to neatly hold back her hair. Ranju looked forward to these birthday parties. She was fascinated by the Khoi-bag tied to the fan, which held so much candy. The hostess would puncture it towards the end of the party and the children scrambled over to grab the goodies. She enjoyed the amazing taste of these sweets. She loved the fancy dress parties too, and most of all, she loved getting her return gifts. Ranju was quite popular with her affluent friends. They liked to play with her and even bullied her at times. But they never visited her shanty. Ranju was never going to invite them home either; she hated her hut and hated being poor.

Mamta continued to fight against the tempest of life with great resilience and determination. Mrs Sareen had made and kept her promise of sending Ranju to a private, English medium school when she turned thirteen. Ranju evinced an air of supremacy over her peers in the slum. She loved rattling off new words to her mother, who smiled and encouraged her passion for learning.

Mamta would often tease Ranju and say, 'I don't understand a word of what you speak, my darling. So maybe you can give me some tuition classes when I'm free in the evenings.'

Ranju had adjusted well in her new school, but remained reticent and struggled to open up to her classmates. She missed her best friend, Pinky. She would rarely meet her except when they bumped into each other in the market.

She only found solace at the riding school. She pursued her riding passionately and soon become an ace rider. As the clock struck four in the afternoon, Ranju would run to help Mrs Verma get the horses ready for the evening class. If any horse hadn't been exercised on a particular day, she would exercise it herself. Mrs Verma had promised to register her for the horse show the following year. She was confident Ranju would walk away with multiple trophies and bring prestige to the school. Impressed by her devotion and dedication to her craft, Mrs Verma was insistent on giving her an equal opportunity to exhibit her skills. Ranju looked elegant when she sat on the horse. She had grown into an attractive, young lady. At fourteen years old, she was tall for her age, and her innocent eyes and childlike demeanour were endearing. She won many hearts with her enthusiasm and hard work at school too.

Even at home, Ranju never shirked from helping her mother clean their little shack or occasionally prepare the evening meal when Mamta was exhausted. She was a pathetic cook and her mother often teased her about it. But Ranju's aspirations were not limited to cooking or cleaning. She strongly craved to take on the world. She would often say, 'I don't want to lead a life just cleaning, cooking and looking after my children. I want to excel and maybe have my own riding school one day, or become a doctor. Ma, I will study hard, and I'm sure I will succeed.'

'Yes, my child, work hard and chart a better future for yourself. Nothing will make me happier.' Mamta certainly didn't want Ranju to lead a life like her own.

If there was one thing mother and daughter had in abundance, it was self-respect.

10

Mamta was returning from work one evening. The heavy rain and incredibly strong winds played havoc with her umbrella. She could not help but get soaked to the bone. Damn this cursed rain, she muttered under her breadth. The monsoons always brought back unwelcome memories of Ram's death. Looking up at the overcast sky, Mamta hastened her pace knowing it wasn't going to stop raining any time soon. Her sari clung to her legs. There weren't any vegetables at home and she knew the vegetable vendor was not going to be around. Ranju abhorred eating just dal, roti or khichri. Mamta prepared herself for another evening of endless grumbling.

She was immersed in her thoughts when she suddenly saw an autorickshaw stop on the opposite side of the road. A man's hand frantically gesticulated to her to get in the auto. She didn't bother to stop and hastened her pace instead. An obscure fear gripped her senses and she continued walking. Maybe, this was a case of mistaken identity. From the corner of her eye she saw the auto take a U-turn and move towards her. Mamta walked on. The auto followed her for ten metres and then she heard the man inside call out her name. She stopped abruptly and tried to make out his face.

'Who is it? I can't see you,' she said, as her voice quivered.

The man stepped out of the auto and took a step towards her. She looked at him, trying to place the familiar figure. He had a plastic bag over his head to protect him from the rain. She stood still, waiting for him to come closer. The wind was pushing her umbrella and she was losing control of it.

'Give it to me and sit inside the auto quickly,' said the man. Mamta recognized the voice instantly. The umbrella slipped from her hand and flew away. The man ran after it, while Mamta stood in the rain unable to move, shell-shocked.

Ganesh had returned after eight long years. Mamta had a lump in her throat and her lower lip trembled as she turned pale. The man, who had deserted her with a million questions left unanswered, was standing in front of her. All those years of despair and humiliation flashed through her mind. The hurtful comments of neighbours and the months of loneliness that had kept her awake night after night. The innumerable days when she had slept on a wet pillow. For years, Mamta hadn't a clue where he was or what had happened to him. She had tried contacting him for months, but his mobile phone was always switched off. She had no answers to the persistent questioning from Gita and Ranju. Above all, it broke her heart when nobody understood her love for this man and judged her with contempt.

Mamta was indignant that Ganesh had the audacity to reappear... for what? Only to make her life miserable again? Gita was finally back to being her best friend and Ganesh had faded away from Ranju's memory and they had learned to live without him.

How could he have the gall to approach me after abandoning me for so many years, Mamta thought to herself. Ganesh hurriedly brought back her umbrella and handed it to her. It was difficult to discern her tears from the raindrops falling on her cheeks. 'Come, I'll drop you home,' he said.

Mamta stepped away from him but he grabbed her arm. She lifted her chin and stood there for a minute gazing into his eyes, her fury knowing no bounds. And then suddenly, she raised her hand and slapped him across the face with all her might. There was no room for any more questions or explanations between them. Pushing him out of her way, she turned on her heels and fled.

Ganesh stood soaking in the rain, shocked. Unable to suppress a shudder, his eyes followed Mamta till he completely lost sight of her. Not surprised by her behaviour, he moved towards the auto, slid inside and slowly removed the polythene bag from his head. He wiped his face with his hands and asked the auto driver to move forward. He knew she was a self-respecting and strong-minded woman, and he had hurt her immensely. To win her back was going to be a colossal task but he had made up his mind.

Mamta reached her shanty sobbing like a little child.

She paced inside for a few moments, venting years of fury and devastation. She flopped on the floor, curled up in a fetal position and cried. Her soul had been completely crushed when Ganesh abandoned them. She had become an emotional wreck and there had been no one to share her sorrow.

'What's the matter, Ma?' Ranju ran and hugged her mother when she walked in half an hour later.

Mamta was too overwhelmed to utter even a single word. She had been discreet and never spoken about Ganesh after he was gone. And now there was no room for him in her life.

'Nothing, darling, just some old memories.'

Leaving her mother to her thoughts, Ranju started making dinner. She looked at her mother from the corner of her eye. What could be the reason for her despair? she thought to herself. Maybe she just had a bad day at work.

Ranju finished cooking khichdi and served her mother a plate. Mamta was emotionally exhausted. She ate quietly and then got into bed and covered her face with a sheet, trying hard to hold back her tears. Ranju could sense the agony in her mother.

'Ma, did you have a rough day at work? Did you have an argument with Gita aunty?'

'I was just missing your father…the rain reminds me of him,' Mamta lied. 'Wash the utensils, please before you go to bed, otherwise they will unnecessarily attract cockroaches,' she said, changing the topic.

Ranju gently caressed her mother's head and then

decided to leave her alone. She washed the utensils, trying to be as quiet as possible. Then she switched off the light and got into bed beside Mamta, laying her hand across her stomach. Mamta turned sideways to embrace her. All they had was only each other in the whole wide world.

Ranju worried for her mother and she also desperately wanted to complete her education and get a job. She disliked her mother working so many shifts, being careless about her diet and never spending an extra penny on herself. Yes, life had been unfair, but Ranju was determined to change their destiny to give her mother much-needed rest and all that she deserved.

Mamta stayed awake and restless that night. Tossing and turning in bed, she thought of her past life and the vacuum in her heart. Ganesh had been a wonderful companion and she had missed him immensely. Had he come back to the city to marry me? Would it be a wise decision to hear him out and give him another chance? Her heart and mind were in turmoil. She wanted him to hold her in his arms and never let go. Eventually when she fell into deep sleep she saw him in her dream. There he was standing with open arms, imploring her to embrace him. She was casting him aside but couldn't resist turning around to look at him every other minute. The road seemed endless. Mamta was exhausted when she woke up next morning. With a firm resolve and a heavy heart, she was emphatic about never seeing Ganesh again. She was not willing to suffer in the hands of a man who had turned his back on her, without a single word.

11

Ganesh too woke up the next morning with Mamta in his thoughts. He knew her morning routine. He hid behind a tree next to the Race Course metro station entrance to catch Mamta dropping Ranju off for school. He waited patiently till she was alone and then accosted her.

'At least listen to what I have to say, Mamta. My family went through a very difficult time and I had to resign to my state of affairs.'

Mamta gave him a dirty look and continued walking away. 'There's nothing left to hear or say.'

Life had been a tough teacher and Mamta had finally learnt to live without Ganesh. She was still attracted to him, but she wasn't ready to succumb to her emotions. Ganesh caught her hand and pulled her to the side of the road, insisting on having a conversation.

'You will have to listen to me Mamta, I still love you,' he said.

Mamta stopped in her tracks, glared at him straight in the eye and said, 'But I don't love you anymore and

I have no interest in what you have to say. Move away or I will have to go to the police station.'

Mamta's feisty response was a revelation for Ganesh. He couldn't believe she had changed so much. He let go of her hand immediately. The last thing he wanted was the police hounding him. He had come back to Delhi to rebuild his life. He did not need to get into any messy situations.

As he walked along with Mamta his thoughts shifted to Ranju. Would she recognise him, or forgive him for his absence? Ganesh had played the role of a perfect father to her. Then abruptly he spun around and crossed the road, to walk on the opposite side. He made the decision to stay away from them for a while and allow her some time to reconcile with his return. There was no point in coercing her to make up with him if she wasn't ready.

Mamta slyly shot him glances from the corner of her eye, making sure he didn't catch her looking at him. They were both walking towards Mrs Sareen's residence. She entered the gate and he followed her inside, but stopped to talk to the new guard. Mamta froze. Was Mrs Sareen planning to replace the current gardener? It would be dreadful to have him breathe down her neck on a daily basis. She had to keep him at arm's length and not fall back into a trap of deceit and sleaze.

A few minutes later, Ganesh walked up to Mrs Sareen, who was sitting in the veranda enjoying her morning orange juice. Mrs Sareen looked up from her newspaper and said, 'What brings you back, Ganesh? You didn't even have the courtesy to inform me that you weren't coming back after your annual leave. If you have come here looking for a job, I already have a gardener. But ask the guard to take you to my neighbour's house. They live four houses away and I believe they are looking for a new gardener.'

Mamta gave a sigh of relief and quickly moved away from behind the living-room door. Her love affair had always been a well-guarded secret at her workplace.

With his new job secured, Ganesh managed to rent a room in the neighbouring slum. He knew Gita's unrelenting hostility would only make his life difficult in DID Colony. He was determined to pursue Mamta as and when he could. He ate his evening meals from roadside dhabas and missed the convenience of Mamta cooking for him. His needed a cycle to commute to work every day, more than buying kitchen utensils and a stove. He knew it would take a month of hardship before he could comfortably settle down. His entire salary had to be sent home every month after the devastation of his village. In order to meet his daily expenses he also washed a few cars every morning before going to work.

The days were easy to endure but evenings were difficult. Ganesh was bored with himself. He would sit with the slum-dwellers in the courtyard outside his shack, discussing politics or other gossip. The smell of alcohol and beedis would often force him to go back inside and sit alone in his hut. Once alone he would think of Mamta, his son Pralad and how Parvati must be coping with life, pushing him to sink into despondency and nostalgia. Soon, Ganesh occasionally helped himself to a drink. It made him sleep better. Drinking every evening became a habit and he enjoyed sitting alone in his shanty with his bottle.

Another reckless habit of his was to follow Mamta every other morning, attempting to persuade her to continue their relationship. She had clearly made up her mind and refused to talk or listen to any explanations.

Mamta knew there was no point in mending fences with a man who held no significance for her anymore. She was an independent, self-respecting woman who had managed to bring her life on track after losing both the men she loved. Her only focus was to ensure Ranju was educated and self-reliant, and she wasn't going to allow her emotions to distract her from her goal. Ganesh had broken her trust and she couldn't allow him to break her heart once again. There was nothing he would do for them, as she had learnt from her past experience. She didn't want to refresh Ranju's memory of him either, nor have any contact with him. He had been away a long time and she was adamant it would stay that way. Mamta was finally at peace with herself.

Ganesh pursued her with determination and failed every time, till eventually he stopped following her or waiting for a glimpse of her. He struggled to accept Mamta's indifference and hoped one day she would forgive him. Now she looked at him with contempt, and their new equation rattled him. He had made a mistake in not staying in touch with her from the village.

It was challenging to hold himself back and not land up in their hut but belittling himself in front of Ranju, a child he had taken care of on so many occasions, was not something he could easily do. Drinking alone in his hut through the night, he occasionally even cried.

12

It was spring and two days from Holi. Ganesh had not been home for nine months and Parvati had managed well without him. It was essential to rebuild their home and save every penny to buy new seeds for the winter crop without wasting a year. Parvati had planted the lemon, strawberry and litchi orchards during the monsoons. Ganesh had outlined his intentions to get into organic farming and start the rotation of crops when he visited the village. He had learnt a great deal in his new job and his enthusiasm to learn had encouraged his employer to often take him to their farms and teach him the basics of organic farming. The opportunity to avail a higher price for organic produce at lower production costs excited him. His desire to buy more land and give his family a better lifestyle drove him to work harder. He took up a part-time job after five pm to earn more and keep himself busy.

Ganesh had just returned to his shanty from the post office after transferring money to Parvati. The cash Holi gift from his employers was enough to help him pull through the month comfortably. He had not seen Mamta for a week now, and he wondered if she was unwell. Their work timings were similar but they walked on opposite sides of the road every day. Mamta refused to even return his greetings if he crossed her path and this humiliated him. All he wanted was to be forgiven, although she was the one who felt let down. His excessive dependence on alcohol only made things worse. There were times when he wanted to appease her and there were times he wanted to harm her. His mind played with devious thoughts when he was drunk, only to calm down when he was sober.

Amid the celebration and festivities of Holi, Ganesh woke up late on his day off. Peeping out of his shack, he saw it was a cloudy morning. It had rained heavily the previous night. He sensed it might pour again and didn't want the rains to dampen a day children awaited all year. His attention instantly drifted to Pralad, who loved playing Holi with him. He smiled to himself and knew his little boy must have slept hugging his pichkari all night. Pralad was the first to jump out of bed on Holi morning and run outside to spray colour on his friends.

Sitting outside his shack, Ganesh waited for his friends to join him. Gradually, they gathered in the courtyard, greeting each other with hugs and a smear of gulal on the forehead. The elders sat watching the children as they played with pichkaris and threw colour-filled balloons at each other. The women had prepared gunjiya, malpua and bhaang to add to the celebrations. By midday Ganesh and his friends were tipsy, and everywhere the eye could see there was jubilation. Ganesh picked up another glass of bhaang despite knowing he had crossed his quota. It was Holi and a couple of extra drinks would do him no harm. He could just retire to his room and sleep after all the fun was over.

By three in the afternoon Ganesh had had plenty to drink. Swaying and slurring, he had to be carried to his room by friends who were as inebriated as him. As he lay down a deep melancholy descended on him. Memories of his father and the devastation of his fields played over in his mind. Pushing those thoughts away, he sat up and poured himself a peg of rum. All he wanted was to rest but sleep had deserted him. He gulped down his drink, wishing it would knock him out, but in vain. Ganesh turned on to his left side facing the wall and Mamta's face flashed through his mind.

Reminiscing about the good old times, he smiled to himself. He desperately wanted to hold her in his arms. The man in him was aroused as he stood up, downed another drink and straggled towards DID Colony. When he reached the slum, he saw the elders assembled around the neem tree still eating, drinking and rejoicing, while the children were screaming and throwing mud at each other. The dholakwalla's exuberance knew no bounds. He was persuading everyone to get up and dance. The only two people missing were Mamta and Ranju. They must be in their shack, he thought. He casually moved towards their hut; nobody recognized him or paid any attention. His face was smeared with colour and he had gained ten kilos over the last few years.

The door to Mamta's shanty was open. Drunk, he

clumsily pushed the door open. The hunger to hold Mamta in his arms had clouded his judgement completely. Mamta wasn't home that morning—she had gone to work as Mrs Sareen had organized a big Holi party at her bungalow. She had requested Mamta to assist with the preparations, which Mamta was more than willing to do. The extra money would help her to purchase a new fridge. Ranju had decided to stay home and study. Holi wasn't her favourite festival. Besides, she didn't have many friends in the slum she could play with.

As he entered the shanty, Ganesh saw Ranju lying on the bed, lost in a deep slumber. He walked up to the bed and looked down at her. Flopping down on the floor next to Ranju, an unexpected malice rose in his heart for Mamta. She had humiliated and insulted him umpteen times, in spite of his efforts to explain his limitations. He had left no stone unturned to tell her how much he loved her, but Mamta had shunned him without exception, finding it below her dignity to even look at him. Overwhelmed by negative emotion, Ganesh's desire to avenge the humiliation and insult, and teach Mamta a lesson clouded all his senses.

He looked at Ranju. He did not see the little girl lying on the bed as his own daughter. He had loved her, looked after her like a father, and had always wished for her wellbeing. But his mind was now darkened with retaliation and alcohol. He cast his family and affections aside. He just wanted revenge.

Ranju's nightdress was raised till her thighs. Ganesh

slowly stroked her leg. Guessing it was her mother, Ranju stirred and rolled over on her stomach. 'How was the party, Ma?' she asked without opening her eyes.

Ganesh stood up, supporting himself against the bed, not stopping to look at her half-exposed bottom. He had not had sex for over nine months. A hateful lust overpowered his sensibilities. He wobbled a bit but managed to pull his pants down. All he wanted was an orgasm. He forcefully rolled Ranju on her back and got on top of her. The little girl was too stunned to react. She opened her eyes in shock and saw a bulky man breathing into her face. She tried pushing him away with all her force and kicked him with all her might. Totally intoxicated, Ganesh lost his balance and fell on the floor, but managed to catch her arm and drag her down as well. Ranju screamed for help, but he smothered her scream with brutal kisses and within a second, he was on top of her again. Ranju was unable to move under his weight, and a sharp pain in her vagina made her lie helplessly on the floor. She tried raising her head but Ganesh had regained his strength. He put his hand over her mouth and pushed her head back. He was hurting her and the excruciating pain was something she had never experienced before. Suddenly everything was pitch-black. Ganesh had not had enough. He stayed on top and did her again. He rolled over after he was spent and lay next to her a few minutes. He then got up abruptly, put on his pants and walked out of the shack without even a look back at Ranju.

Ranju gained consciousness after a while and found

she was lying on the floor, unable to move. She couldn't understand what had happened to her. Why was she in so much pain and what had that man done to her? She sat up slowly, leaning against the bed. Pulling her nightdress down she held the seam close to her ankles. She sat there for a long time, speechless and dazed, not knowing what to do. Time was dragging its feet and her mother was taking forever to come home. She stood up slowly to bolt the door and felt her body convulsing with every step she took. Wincing with pain, she sat on the edge of her bed.

Mamta glanced at the watch in the kitchen. It was nearly five in the evening. She had a plastic bag full of leftover food from the party and was relieved she wouldn't have to cook that night. Ranju relished the papri chaat, pav bhaji and rasmalai. Walking towards her shanty, Mamta saw Gita sitting under the neem tree.

'We missed you this morning, but I have saved some gunjiya and malpua for you,' Gita said with a broad smile.

'I've brought some rasmalai for you too,' replied Mamta, handing over a plastic packet to her. Both women had become closer in recent years, and Gita and Jagdish were her only support system. They walked leisurely towards Gita's shanty, chatting about the big party at Mrs Sareen's. Mamta was curious to know if Ranju had joined the Holi frolic.

'She didn't come out at all and was busy studying or watching TV, I suppose. I did ask her but did not insist, since she doesn't like playing Holi anyway,' replied Gita.

Ranju's diligence made her mother proud and she knew that soon enough their difficulties would be a thing of the past.

Mamta walked home happily, anticipating Ranju's excitement at opening the boxes to devour her favourite sweets and snacks. Surprised to find the door locked from inside, Mamta called out for Ranju. She stood outside impatiently, and with no response after a while, she once again called out loudly, 'Ranju, hurry up, my arms are aching carrying these heavy packets of food.'

Ranju could hear her mother but she just stared at the door, inert. A fear had gripped her senses and her head was spinning like a ceiling fan. She hesitantly walked to the door and stood there for a few seconds, before she could get herself to open it. Mamta didn't notice anything wrong and walked in without looking at Ranju.

'For how long have you been sleeping? Didn't you study at all?' she asked while opening the packets of food with her back towards Ranju.

Talking about the party with her daughter she did not notice Ranju just standing by the door, stupefied. She looked at her mother with tear-filled eyes, staggered over to her and clung to her back, crying uncontrollably. Mamta caught unawares, immediately spun around.

'What's happened, Ranju?' she asked in panic.

Ranju's crying was unstoppable, and she didn't answer her. She had no idea how to express what had happened to her, or why a stranger had hurt her so brutally. She kept crying without saying a word. Mamta's fears knew no bounds.

'What's the problem, Ranju? I'm going to call Gita aunty,' she said.

'Don't leave me alone, Ma,' Ranju clung to her mother and screamed.

Mamta pushed her back and looked at her daughter. She noticed a bruise at the corner of her mouth. Her brows were knit together and her eyes had a fear in them which Mamta had never seen before. Ranju crossed both her arms across her chest. Mamta could see her fingers tremble and blue marks across her left wrist. It struck her that her Ranju might have been molested. She pushed Ranju aside and ran to Gita's shack. Gita and Jagdish were drinking their evening tea when she barged in unannounced.

'Come out quickly, Gita! Leave your tea and hurry up.'

Gita knew at once that something was drastically wrong. Mamta was a usually calm person. She instantly left her cup of tea and ran after her. Jagdish offered to come along but Mamta refused. Gita panicked when she saw Ranju: her hair in disarray, her eyes swollen and her ghostly white complexion. It sent a shiver down Gita's spine. Ranju looked anything but normal. Gita looked at Mamta and said, 'I think she needs a doctor.'

As they held Ranju and helped her walk to the bed, Gita spotted some blood stains on the floor and bent down to check. Mamta looked at the stains and then at Gita. Both women knew at once Ranju had been raped. They both stared at each other in shock and disbelief.

'Did someone come to the hut?' Mamta shouted as loud as she could.

'Yes, Ma. Someone I don't know. His face was covered with colour and I couldn't recognize him,' Ranju quivered in pain.

Mamta sank to the floor and bawled like a child, while Gita stood rooted, staring at the mother and daughter too stunned to react.

Gita regained her composure. 'Let's go to the police station at once. There is nothing else we can do.'

She immediately ran back to her shanty and informed Jagdish, who advised them against it. 'There's no point in making any complaint unless we have a person to complain against. Let's give Ranju some time, after which she might be able to tell us who it was. If he was someone from the slum, Ranju could recognize him but for now, let's wait. Going without any evidence will only bring us shame. Let's take care of Ranju right now and not mention anything to anyone. There is no need to encourage gossip,' suggested Jagdish.

'What are you saying, Jagdish bhai? My daughter has been raped and I want to make a police complaint!' Mamta said between her tears. 'How can I let this just pass? Please take us to the police station right away. I won't be able to forgive myself otherwise.'

'Be sensible, Mamta. The police can be very cruel. They will end up blaming Ranju and you. We should wait and ask her again tomorrow morning. She is very young and won't be able to handle the police inquiries.'

'No, bhai, I can't let this pass!" she screamed back. Jagdish was a mature, sensible man and knew he had to handle this tactfully.

'Mamta, don't bring shame on yourself and ruin Ranju's life forever. It is better we keep this a secret. You know how the neighbours reacted to Ganesh. Please, I request you for now just keep this quiet...let's focus on Ranju.'

Following this advice, Mamta was resigned to keep their sorrow a firmly-guarded secret. That night, Mamta and Ranju slept clinging to each other, trying very hard to keep their spirits alive.

Ganesh woke up before the crack of dawn at three, feeling squeamish and nervous. Swallowed by guilt, he was finding it impossible to concentrate on anything. He lay in bed for a while, feeling agitated and then got out of bed, restlessly pacing up and down the room. In one moment of madness, he had committed the most heinous sin. He swore never to drink again. He loved Mamta and had never intended to do anything to harm her daughter.

He walked hurriedly to the top of the road for some fresh air. As a passerby stopped him to ask for directions, Ganesh was startled, and found himself stuttering and stammering. He was being unusually paranoid. What if someone had recognized him? What if the police came knocking on his door in the morning? How would his family manage if he went to jail?

He didn't want to face anyone or even think about Mamta and Ranju. Ganesh promptly ran back to his shanty and threw his clothes into the suitcase, hoping to catch the first train to his village. No one around him knew where he came from. His employer hadn't even asked for his ID proof. Ganesh sent a quick message to his landlord, saying his mother was seriously ill and he left the room rent and keys on the bed before leaving for the railway station. He didn't want anyone looking for him. Ganesh had made up his mind to leave—it wasn't possible to live in Delhi anymore. He left for his village carrying his shameful secret with him, never to return.

13

Ranju woke up the next morning terrified. She didn't want to leave her bed and Mamta stayed home to be with her. Gita also informed both her employers that she would be on leave for the next three–four days. Who could have been responsible for Ranju's rape? There was no one in DID Colony they could point a finger at. The questions kept haunting Mamta, but she didn't want to make Ranju relive her traumatic experience again and again.

Gita came to visit them in the morning carrying some lunch. The packets from Mrs Sareen's party lay half-unpacked and smelled foul, but Mamta and Ranju were too distraught to notice. Gita removed the stale food and put a plate of fresh khichri in front of them. Ranju silently sat on the bed, slouched next to her mother, with her fists clenched and eyes fixed on the floor. As Mamta put a spoonful in her mouth, Ranju ate feebly, taking intervals. She still had stabbing pain in her crotch, all the way down to her legs. She'd lift her drooped eyelids every now and then to look at her mother. All Mamta could do was give her a half-reassuring smile and put her arm around her, forming a protective shield. For Mamta this was even worse than losing Ram.

'You'll be better, my child,' said Gita, as tears welled in her eyes. They knew they had to be committed to Ranju to help her heal.

Ranju had been sexually assaulted by a stranger, and not one of them could do anything to get her justice. The family had to swallow this terrible violation like a bitter pill. Ranju could not sleep for the next few nights as fear clutched at her throat with its cold fingers. Even when she dozed off from sheer exhaustion, she would wake up in a cold sweat, having relived her assault. During the daytime, the flashbacks were so vivid that she would wrap herself up with a bedsheet wanting protection from the predator. She felt mortified and dirty, as though she had been marked for life. Her emotional state swayed between intense pain and numbness. Her anxiety at nights would manifest in physical symptoms. She would often find it difficult to breathe, her muscles would tense up and the stomach cramps would force her to scream in pain.

Mamta felt helpless as a mother, but she knew she had to talk to Ranju and help her recover. It was important for her to go back to school, so she might occupy herself with other things. Ranju hadn't left her room for four days and would drag her mother along even when she had to go to the toilet. She would sleep clinging to her mother and Mamta could feel her daughter soaked with sweat, breathing heavily and suddenly sitting up in bed, crying hysterically. This could not carry on any longer.

It was necessary to get her out of the house and restart her life again.

'Let's go for a walk, Ranju. The weather is beautiful outside and you need a little change,' said Mamta, and Ranju reluctantly agreed.

It was a Sunday evening and the sun seemed like a disk of gold. The sky was tinged with different hues of yellow and orange, and the air was fresh. Huge trees lined the roads with the birds chirping away. People had stepped out for their evening walk and some were strolling with their pets.

'We have to be brave, my girl, and fight this together. We are poor and cannot afford the luxury of not going to work. I will have to go back to Mrs Sareen's and the riding school, and you should start going to school too. This secret has to be kept in our hearts forever and we have to reclaim our lives together.'

Ranju didn't say a word, but nodded silently.

The next morning, Mamta was up early as usual and ready to leave for the stable, when she found Ranju sitting quietly on the bed.

'I don't want to be alone, Ma. Can I come along with you?' she asked and Mamta agreed.

They both reached the riding school together and Mrs Verma welcomed them with a smile.

'My, my! Look who is here this beautiful morning. Where have you been, Ranju? I missed you so much. Come help me with the horses,' she said, extending her arm towards the child.

Mamta and Ranju exchanged glances as Mamta disappeared into the kitchen and Ranju followed Mrs Verma into her office. After she finished her work, they rushed back home and Ranju slowly got ready for school. Gita was sitting under the neem tree and offered to accompany them to the metro station. The trio walked in silence. When they reached the station Mamta couldn't hide her anxiety and said, 'Ranju, please don't worry about anything and be careful not to talk to any strangers. I'll get you a mobile phone tomorrow,which you can carry to school.'

Ranju looked hesitant but walked down the stairs one at a time, turning around every now and then to get a comforting nod from her mother. She felt vulnerable and unsafe, gripped by the fear of being alone. The station was crowded and she was judging every man with hostility, fearing her adversary would reappear and harm her again. She now viewed herself and the world differently. She felt compelled to see every man with suspicion, not trusting anyone who stood next to her. For a young girl of thirteen years it was difficult to understand her trauma. The only person she could trust was her mother and she wanted to be back in her arms. She sat on a bench, waiting quietly for the train. When it arrived Ranju couldn't get herself to move. A couple of trains went by and a burly man came and sat next to her, waiting for his train. Ranju's throat turned dry with fear and she hurriedly ran up the stairs and out of the station and continued running till she reached home. Once home, she bolted the door and sat in a corner waiting for her mother to return.

'Don't worry, Ranju. We'll leave a bit early every morning and I'll drop you to school and pick you up myself. I'll request Mrs Sareen and adjust my timings accordingly for a few days,' Mamta pacified Ranju when she got home.

Mamta had to be strong in order to give Ranju the much-required support. It wasn't a time to be weak and Mamta had to brush aside her feelings of despair and march forward. She missed Ram like never before but was helpless in this hour of crisis.

Ranju woke up the next morning and announced with conviction, 'I will study in my old school, near the house,' she said.

Mamta was deeply anxious and tried gently cajoling her daughter. 'Your future depends on your education, my girl. Be sensible and please don't let this incident spoil your future. There's a long road ahead of you and there is so much to look forward to.' She tried to persuade Ranju every morning for a week, but she was adamant and Mamta had to finally relent.

She managed to enrol Ranju back in her old school. Pinky was happy to have her friend back, but soon realized that Ranju was a completely different person. She hardly spoke to anyone and preferred to sit by herself most of the time. She waited for her mother after school and didn't want to walk home alone or with Pinky. No matter how hard she tried to overcome her ordeal, Ranju constantly felt jumpy and unsure. The assault was not only an invasion of her physical self but also her intellectual, social and emotional being. The unfortunate incident had destroyed her self-confidence and changed her perception about the world—and her place in it. She was depressed, restless and often confused and angry.

Mamta was extremely worried about Ranju's health. She even discussed it with Gita and Jagdish, who consoled her. Ranju even stopped going to the riding school, even though Mrs Verma personally came to talk to her.

'You are an ace rider, Ranju, and I have great expectations from you. What's the matter with you, my girl, why this sudden change of heart?' she asked. But Mamta wasn't inclined to confide in anyone.

Days turned into weeks and then into months, but Ranju didn't go back to the riding school. Mamta had lost touch with Ram's family, her own father had passed away and she wasn't close enough to her brother to ask for help. She was hesitant about taking Ranju back to the village. Times were tough and Mamta had to deal with her tribulations alone. Ranju was taking time to heal and stayed aloof. Keeping her distracted was daunting.

One night around eight pm, Mamta was preoccupied, tossing the aloo bhindi on the stove and fretting for Ranju, when she suddenly spun around and asked, 'Ranju, I haven't bought you any pads for so long. Haven't you had your period?'

'No, Ma. They've stopped thankfully,' Ranju replied innocently, watching Indian Idol on the TV.

Mamta gawked stood up at once, realizing that her daughter was pregnant. How could I be so careless? A shiver ran down her spine. Now she had to face the world with an unwanted infant born of rape.

Mamta could smell the aloo bhindi burning and as she tried taking the pan off the stove with her bare hands she dropped it. Ranju quickly reached for the mop to help clean up.

'I'll take you to the doctor tomorrow morning,' said Mamta. She first needed confirmation. She prayed all night, wishing for the Gods to show her some mercy. The next morning, Mamta hurriedly rushed Ranju to the doctor.

'Your daughter is pregnant,' the doctor announced and Mamta's fears came true.

'Can she have an abortion?'

'Ranju is over five months pregnant and it could be dangerous.'

Besides it was against the law to abort after twenty weeks, unless the pregnancy endangered the woman's life or the child had a grave physical or mental disability.

Over the next few weeks, Mamta had to brace herself to explain and prepare Ranju for her pregnancy. Emotions ran high.

'I don't want this baby, Ma,' Ranju shouted.

'Ranju, we have to accept this baby as our own, and you have to love your child like I love you. We can't do anything now and I'm not going to take any risks with your life.'

For several days, Mamta tried pacifying her daughter, but Ranju was completely unrelenting. She was not going to change her mind. She did not want to have this baby against her will. When all efforts failed, Mamta and Gita decided to leave her alone and give her time to think it over, and hope Ranju would accept and understand her responsibilities as the days went by.

Wondering about the days ahead, Mamta anticipated having to fend off slanderous remarks from her neighbours while taking care of a pregnant Ranju and her newborn child. She often discussed her predicament with Gita, who promised to protect Ranju and support the family. 'You can't send Ranju to school, as it will be really disconcerting for her. Children can be very cruel,' Gita told Mamta. She knew it was going to be a Herculean job to explain anything to Ranju but she was the only one who could do it.

'Ranju, my princess... You are going to be a mother and it's something none of us wanted. However, the sad reality is that we have no choice but to have this baby. If we had known earlier, we would have definitely got it aborted. Just be a sensible girl and don't trouble your mother. You can't go to school from tomorrow. You need to just look after yourself and help me with the house work. Just remember to keep the door bolted at all times or go to Gita aunty's if you like.'

Ranju started at her mother without saying a word. All her aspirations had been crushed by a stranger and she could do nothing to change her situation. She would never go to school again or live the life of a regular teenager. Her life would be worse than her mother's and her ambitions had come to an abrupt end. The hours she spent on her studies and riding practice had gone down the drain. She stormed out of her hut and Gita followed her. Gita held her hand, took her to the neem tree and sat her down.

'You can go back to school once the baby is born and you are a bit older. Right now we are stuck, Ranju, and can't risk your life. Please understand your mother's pain.'

'You all are horrible,' Ranju screamed.

'We love you, Ranju, and want the best for you.'

Ranju knew it was pointless to keep fighting.

Over the next few months, she retreated into a shell and totally lost her self-esteem. She would sit under the neem tree, pondering and building hatred for her child who was yet to be born. In moments of utter desperation, Ranju would hit her stomach violently or jump up and down, hoping to smother her child. She hated herself just as much as she hated her unborn child. She lost her appetite and would stay up all night, thinking about her meaningless life and cursing her very existence. She also felt isolated and was unable to share her feelings even with her mother.

Mamta on the other hand had reconciled with their terrible destiny and felt deeply sorry for Ranju. But she could do nothing except to try and reassure her. She knew that her daughter's dreams for a higher education and a better life had been brutally shattered.

14

Ranju gave birth to a baby girl on a cold winter day. Seeing her granddaughter for the first time, Mamta hesitated and then kissed her forehead. It was difficult to shake the uncanny resemblance of the child to Ganesh. For a fraction of a second, Mamta thought whether Ganesh was responsible for this heinous act, but she promptly pushed her suspicions aside. Ganesh had been an ideal father to Ranju. She hadn't seen or thought of him for months

Back in his village, Ganesh was safe and secure with his family and farming business. Although he was haunted by his guilt, he had resolved to never cross Mamta or Ranju's path any time in the future. He would take his secret to his grave.

Little Maya came as a ray of sunshine into Mamta's miserable life. Untouched by the sin that had brought her to life, Maya was innocent and beautiful like a morning daisy. Ranju had been in labour with her for nearly two days. Looking at her delicate fingers, her divine eyes and smooth flawless skin, Mamta would overlook the agony and misfortune of their lives. Irrespective of all the darkness they were engulfed in, Mamta would dream of what this little child could grow up to be. As a million questions and possibilities ran through her mind, Mamta realized it was their job to raise this baby to the best of their ability and make sure she was untouched by the circumstances of her birth.

Ranju, on the other hand, felt no affection towards the little girl. She felt nauseated when she saw the tiny body in a cot next to her and was dispassionate as the child wailed loudly into her ears. Maya quivered with stomach gripes and her entire body became rigid with hunger, but Ranju was implacable, till the nurse rushed into the room and reprimanded Ranju.

'The baby is hungry and needs to be fed,' the nurse uttered annoyed.

'I hate this child and I am not going to feed her,' Ranju reiterated.

The nurse looked at her flabbergasted, but did not say a word. She understood how mothers sometimes reacted negatively after enduring labour pains for hours.

'I can't spend all day trying to coax you,' she said irritably. The general ward was crowded and the noisy chatter was wearing the nurse down. She had no time to pander to Ranju or her emotions.

Ranju turned her face away. She had grudgingly given birth to this child but her heart was impenetrable. She held the innocent child accountable for invading her life and crushing all her desires to pulp. She could do nothing to reclaim her life.

Disgruntled at her apathy, the nurse took the baby away from her. She walked Maya up and down the corridor, sang to her and cuddled her, but the baby was hungry and had to be fed. When Mamta returned to the general ward after settling the bills and heard the child wailing incessantly, she was appalled at Ranju.

'Be sensible, Ranju, and feed your baby. You're her mother and the little child is hungry,' said Mamta.

'I abhor this child and I will not feed her. Let her die for all I care.' Her mother stared in disbelief.

Mamta tried to coax her, but Ranju was unwilling to take the baby in her arms. Finally little Maya had to be given a bottle. Mamta hoped that Ranju's selfish attitude would soften once they returned home.

No one in the slum believed Ranju had been raped, as no police complaint had been filed. People were quick to judge her and accused her of being as loose as her mother. Gita and Jagdish did everything in their power to make Ranju and her baby feel welcome, but no one else cared. They wanted Mamta and Ranju to move out of the slum and their constant hostility was hard to endure. Ranju's hostile attitude was making things worse, but Mamta had made up her mind that she was never going to move elsewhere. She had lived here from the very first day she came to Delhi with Ram. The slum-dwellers tried persuading her landlord, but he lived far away and hardly ever visited DID Colony. Besides, his rent was never delayed and Mamta made sure to give him his ten percent increment when he demanded it. Mamta was a good tenant and he didn't want to lose her.

Two weeks passed by and Ranju was still stubborn.

'Do you think we should put the baby in an orphanage?' Gita asked Mamta one morning.

Mamta flatly rejected this suggestion. 'I will raise her like my own daughter. I can never part with my grandchild. Let's hope time heals Ranju's scars and she accepts her daughter one day.'

For days and nights, Ranju stayed cooped up in her shack till the baby's persistent crying coerced her to go and sit quietly in Mrs Verma's riding school, brooding over her misery. Mrs Verma felt sorry for Ranju. She had been her favourite student and had an unparallel zeal to pursue her interests. It was painful to see her future shattered to pieces. She often coaxed Ranju, 'It's not the end of the world, my child. You should come and start riding again. I understand your situation, but you have to face your adversities. Don't worry about a thing, we are all with you.'

Ranju was reluctant to face the world. She felt naked when she stepped out of her shack. She was ashamed of her secret and feared that people would blame her and judge her character. No one in the slum had spared her their taunts and sniggers.

Weeks passed but Ranju's maternal instincts did not kick in and Maya's entire responsibility fell on Mamta's shoulders. She loved her granddaughter and wasn't in the least perturbed about bringing her up by herself. She would bathe, change and feed her when she was home and when she was out, Gita would watch her. Mamta's exhaustion did surface at times, but Ranju would only sit and watch, not once offering to help. She would help with the house work occasionally, but doing anything for Maya seemed impossible. Her anger and resentment towards Maya was most apparent at nights, when she was unable to sleep for more than a few hours. She would often have violent thoughts and scream things like 'Get this nuisance out of our shack or I'll throw her into the drain when you go to work.' Mamta would usually ignore her behaviour, but she worried for Maya and her future.

As time went by Ranju's hatred for Maya grew. Her anger for the anonymous man who had destroyed her life was feeding this hatred. She knew her future was bleak and her insecurities crippled her heart and mind. She felt miserable and lonely, she had no friends in the neighbourhood. She didn't want to engage with anyone either, and whenever she stepped out, she simply ignored people, without paying heed to their jibes.

Ranju was convinced that if this child was out of her way, she might start leading a normal life once again. Gita aunty had promised she could go back to school, and she planned to restart her riding classes as well. It had been over a year since the horrible incident, and she soon came to realize that Gita aunty did not really mean what she said to console her back then. Recognizing this, Ranju's bitterness went up a few notches and her rancour towards Maya ballooned. Marriage and men were never going to be a part of her life. She could not trust any man. With time, the nightmares had become less frequent, but Ranju was still traumatized. She would wake up at nights, drenched in a cold sweat and resenting everyone and everything around her.

Maya was an adorable child, with an effervescent smile like her grandmother. She had taken the best from her family. She was tall like her grandfather, had her grandmother's affable nature and the best features from her mother. Despite their resentment and hostility, the slum-dwellers couldn't help but fall in love with this little girl. Maya would play happily under the neem tree while Gita watched over her. Ranju would scream and roughly push her aside whenever she crossed her path. The child couldn't decipher why this woman, whom she called 'Mummy', was so uncaring towards her. She was scared of Ranju and stayed out of her way as much as she could. Gita pondered if Ranju would ever overcome her misery and accept her daughter wholeheartedly.

As the days went by, Ranju would sit under the neem tree and think of how she could get rid of Maya forever. One warm afternoon, when Mamta had gone to work and Gita had dozed off under the neem tree, Ranju found an opportunity to avenge her pain and remove Maya from their lives forever. Her hatred overpowered all motherly instincts as she caught Maya's arm and dragged her toward their shack.

'Nani is calling you, come home immediately,' she lied and pulled Maya with all her might.

Maya lost her balance and was dragging herself along her mother's feet, tears gushing down her face and blurring her vision. The little girl was scared to even let out a scream. She had been slapped, pinched and pulled mercilessly by Ranju in the past for crying or throwing child-like tantrums. For Maya, her mother was like a demon. Ranju threw her down on the bed. Not knowing what to do next, she stood there staring at the child. Maya tried getting off the bed but Ranju pinned her down and gave her a tight slap.

Then she picked up a pillow lying nearby and smothered Maya's face with it, trying to suffocate her. All that the little child could do was kick her feet and gasp for breath. Ranju pressed the pillow on her face with all her might. After a few seconds, when Maya stopped kicking and her coughs started to fade, Ranju suddenly found herself being violently pulled away. She fell on the bed, hitting her head against the wall and saw Gita standing right behind her.

'What are you trying to do?' Gita screamed. She picked up Maya in her arms and stared at Ranju, stunned.

'I hate this child and I'm ashamed of her. She is the cause of my misery and I cannot forgive her for ruining my life.'

Gita had nothing to say. She understood Ranju's frustration, but this was certainly not the way to deal with it.

It was now apparent that Ranju could not be trusted around Maya. Gita waited for Mamta to get home, petrified at the thought of what could have happened.

'Luckily I woke up in time and ran to your shack when I found Maya missing. If I was a few minutes late, Ranju would have murdered her and all of us could have been in the police station right now,' said Gita.

Mamta was dumbstruck.

'Ranju is becoming dangerous, Gita, and I don't know how to handle her. She might try doing this again.' Mamta sat huddled with Gita in her shanty, waiting for Jagdish to return.

Back in her house, Ranju was miserable that she had failed to remove Maya from her life. She had no remorse at all. For Ranju, Maya was a painful reminder of her trauma and the faster she was out of the way the better. She was lying in bed staring at the ceiling, when Mamta stormed into the shack with Maya in her arms. She put her down on the bed, went up to Ranju and slapped her hard across her face.

Shouting at the top of her voice, she told Ranju in no uncertain terms that her actions were unequivocally despicable. Distraught by her behaviour, Mamta and Jagdish were adamant that Ranju start working. Sitting at home, doing nothing except feeding negativity would be dangerous for all of them.

Ranju had no desire to work as a safaiwali. 'You have already ruined my life by forcing me to have this child. Now I cannot do anything to turn my life around.

Stop ordering me to be a servant in someone's house!' she said, belligerent.

Ranju did not believe her mother when she said that her life would have been in danger had she gone for an abortion when she was five months' pregnant. She was now seventeen years old, and did not understand the repercussions of what she had attempted. Her universe had crumbled even before she could learn to face the world. She was still scared to leave her home alone. Mamta looked at her daughter and suddenly felt a lump in her throat. She felt sorry for her, but it was important that Ranju kept herself busy and earned her own livelihood.

'Jagdish uncle will find you a good job. It's time for you to start leading a sensible life. There is a world outside the four walls of our shack,' she said firmly.

Jagdish's employer had been looking for a personal maid and he recommended Ranju for the job. 'My madam is often unwell and is looking for a caretaker. Besides, I will be around to keep an eye on you. You will be safe,' he said.

Ranju avoided eye contact with Jagdish and was conscious of not breaking into an argument with her mother in his presence. She had no objection to working for Mrs Sareen or Mrs Verma, so she could be close to her mother.

'There is no vacancy at Mrs Sareen's house or Mrs Verma's stable. You must go with Jagdish uncle,' Mamta said.

Jagdish intervened, 'She is offering a nine-to-six job,

with lunch. You will be busy all day and also earn some good money.'

Mamta wanted Ranju to go with Jagdish and get out of her comfort zone. Ranju tried to wriggle her way out of the situation, but Mamta was persistent. Ranju remained stubborn until Jagdish, without mincing any words, firmly warned Ranju, 'We find it unsafe to leave Maya with you for a single minute and if you don't listen to us, we will be forced to tell the police about what you did last night.'

Mamta recognized that his intention was not to threaten her, but they had to get Ranju to leave the slum and go out to work in a better environment. Ranju had no choice but to quietly follow Jagdish to her new employer's residence the next day. She sulked all the way, answering Jagdish only in monosyllables and resenting him for bullying her. Mamta realized that Ranju may not be ready, but shielding her all the time was not in her own interest. As a mother she had to do what was best for her.

Ranju walked in to Mrs Banerjee's bungalow and saw a fleet of servants waiting on her. Mrs Banerjee instantly liked Ranju and felt sorry for her. The innocence in her eyes won her heart straight away. Ranju's employer was a gentle and compassionate soul who overindulged her staff and went out of her way to help them. She affectionately put her arm around Ranju and led her to the study.

'I know you have never worked before, but my retiring maid will teach you everything and you will become an expert within a month.'

Ranju just sat on the floor, with her eyes fixed on

her fingers, fidgeting nervously with them. 'I don't know anything about you except that Jagdish says he's known you since you were a child,' Mrs Banerjee said, trying to cajole her to speak. But Ranju didn't respond and continued playing with her fingers. All she wanted was to scream and tell Mrs Banerjee she didn't want to work in her house or be around people. She just wanted to be left alone.

'Are you married?' Mrs Banerjee probed.

Ranju just nodded her head to say no, without looking up. She wasn't going to share her life story with someone she had just met.

'Alright then. Just follow my maid around for a week and she will help you learn the work. Don't hesitate to ask if you need something.'

There was an undeniable comfort Ranju felt with Mrs Banerjee, but the idea of walking alone to work and walking back, being surrounded by so many unknown people was weighing her down. She remained sulky all day and didn't say a word to anyone. On her way home, Ranju appealed to Jagdish never to disclose Maya's identity to anyone.

He rested his hand on her head and said, 'I promise I won't tell anyone. Also, you will be very happy with Mrs Banerjee. Anyone who comes to work here holds on to their job and leaves only when they retire. It's very easy to keep Mrs Banerjee pleased as she is a gem of a person. You must leave your past behind and look forward to a new beginning.'

Ranju looked at Jagdish, smiled and walked away toward her shanty.

'Did you like your new madam?' Mamta asked her. Ranju was still brooding and resented her mother crowding her space.

'Do I have a choice?' She got up to leave the shack.

'If you don't change your attitude, Ranju, you won't be able to work for anybody. Nobody cares about a sulk.'

Ranju ignored her mother and walked out of their hut defiantly. Mamta had unknowingly given her ammunition which she was sure to use the next day at work. When Ranju returned to the shack, she saw Maya crying.

'What is the matter with her? She is getting on to my nerves,' Ranju screamed, as Maya hid behind her grandmother. Mamta berated Ranju for being inconsiderate towards the little girl. She picked Maya up and hugged her, while Maya clung to her grandmother, scared she might be attacked again.

'Don't blame this child for anything, because it's not her fault. It's your duty to give your child all the love she deserves.'

'You should have let me die, Ma, than have this noose around my neck every waking moment.'

Ranju went to work grudgingly the next morning and exploited the ammunition her mother had given her all day. She sulked endlessly, desperately trying to put off her employer. She was intimidated by the male servants but found solace in having Jagdish around.

Within a week, Ranju sadly realized that everybody

accepted her grumpy face as part of her temperament. She now trudged along with Jagdish every morning without speaking a single word.

She liked Mrs Banerjee, talking to her while she was around her bedroom, but was wary when probed about her life at home. Within a month of going to work, Mamta was relieved to see an improved Ranju. She would eagerly wake up in the morning to get ready and seemed happy when she came home. She still never missed an opportunity to scold Maya. Buying her gifts from her salary was out of the question. She did contribute towards the household expenses.

Mamta ignored her indifference and did whatever she thought was best for both the children. Maya was the apple of her eye and she would buy her little gifts from the extra money she saved up every month. Ranju didn't care at all to think about her daughter's future, but her additional salary had changed their lives for the better.

Maya was an obedient child and seldom threw tantrums or made any demands. She had started going to school and enjoyed her time there. She was popular with her friends, and her teachers adored her. She was a brilliant student and her eagerness to learn would often surprise her teachers. Mamta loved picking her up from school and derived great pleasure in receiving compliments from her teachers and other parents. Maya was sensible and mature for her years and regularly stood by the playground, watching the senior boys play cricket or football.

'This child has tremendous potential and you must enrol her in a good school,' her class teacher told a beaming Mamta one afternoon. Mamta now had all her hopes on little Maya's shoulders, waiting for her to grow up and make a better life for herself.

15

Two Years Later

Mamta lay in bed, burning with fever and a severe headache, while Maya sat next to her soaking her forehead with a wet cloth. She was five years old and her little hands could barely squeeze out the water. Gita dropped by every other hour to check on her best friend. Ranju had moved into Mrs Banerjees's house as a full-time maid and only visited her family once a week.

'I need to see a doctor urgently. Please call Gita nani,' Mamta whispered to Maya.

She was unable to lift her head from the pillow and her condition seemed to be deteriorating. Gita immediately took her to a hospital. Mrs Sareen asked her family doctor to attend to Mamta, but she died a week later, after an attack of bacterial meningitis.

Her death was a blow to Ranju. She was hysterical and unable to come to terms with her mother's sudden demise. Maya was too young to fathom the gravity of the situation. She quietly approached her mother and sat next to her, but Ranju just elbowed her away.

'Stop clinging to me, you ill-fated girl,' she snarled. Gita gently pulled Maya away and sat her on her lap.

Ranju made up her mind to shift to Mrs Banerjee's house permanently. Who would look after little Maya? Her future was now in jeopardy. Gita and Jagdish were exceedingly worried about her. Ranju was a dangerous and irresponsible mother and they couldn't take Maya's responsibility forever. They asked Ranju to move back to the slum and share Maya's supervision.

'I will never move back. Why don't you put her in an orphanage? I don't want her and you can't look after her. She's shattered all my dreams. I'm too old to go back to school or ride again because of this one,' retorted Ranju.

It was heart-wrenching for Gita to see Ranju's unabated revulsion for her own daughter, even under such severe circumstances. Ranju had no one she could call her own, but the very mention of Maya made her angry, like a raging bull. She reiterated that she would have no part to play in Maya's upbringing and she would stay on at Mrs Banerjee's.

'For how long can I share my bed with Maya? We have to find a permanent solution. We are also getting old and have to secure her future before something happens to us too,' said Gita.

"Are you unwilling to even pay the rent for your shanty? The landlord hasn't asked for last month's rent yet, but how long can you survive on sympathy and charity?'

'I'm not the author of my misfortunes and please

stop coming back to me with the same request. I don't want to be reminded of that horrible incident every single minute. Maya will play no role in my life and I have finally reconciled with my fate, with great difficulty.'

'We can't throw Maya out of the window like an old toy. I understand what happened to you was the most frightening and unfortunate experience of your life. I wish I could change the truth but sadly, I can't. You have been mistreating Maya for far too long and now it's time to put things straight,' Jagdish admonished her.

Gita decided to hold onto Mamta's hut for another month hoping Ranju would have a change of heart. Maya often ran into her old home and hugged her Nani's salwar kameez still hanging behind the door. How much she missed her warmth, her cuddles, her kisses and now her protection. She spent hours sitting next to the stove, where her Nani diligently cooked for the family every day, and cried not knowing what was happening with her life.

A month passed by but Ranju did not relent. So Jagdish finally went to discuss the situation with Mrs Sareen. After all, Mamta had worked with her for so many years.

Mrs Sareen promised to sponsor Maya's education in a good school and provide for her basic necessities, but who would take care of her and where would she live? Unable to find a solution, Jagdish finally threw his hands up in the air and went straight to Mrs Banerjee, swearing her to secrecy. After listening to the entire story, Mrs Banerjee finally understood why Ranju had her defences up all the time.

'Rape is the worst experience any woman can go through. Trauma and suffering for so many years is inevitable. Let's hope she finds ways to make friends with the world again soon,' Mrs Banerjee said. 'Ranju has already told me she has no one to fall back on and wants to stay with me permanently. It's obvious she wants to have nothing to do with Maya and now I too believe that Maya won't be safe with her.

'I know a family who is looking for adoption. I have told them everything about Ranju and Maya, and they are willing to consider adopting Maya,' she said. The couple, Shalini and Rajan Malhotra, had been married for over ten years and had lost all hope of having a biological child of their own. They had been considering the option of adopting. Rajan and Shalini were blessed with all the luxuries and comforts of life, but their family was incomplete without an offspring.

Jagdish's happiness was boundless. He gave Mrs Banerjee a wide smile and thanked her with folded hands. The relief was apparent on his face.

'They don't want to meet her at their residence and would prefer to meet her here, but Ranju is around all the time and doesn't even go on her weekly holidays anymore,' said Mrs Banerjee candidly.

Jagdish thought for a moment and came up with an idea, 'You can send her for a few hours to your daughter's house.'

'That's a good idea.'

Two weeks later, she called Ranju and said, 'You will

be going to Jiah's house to help with her son's birthday party. They need a helper and Jiah has especially asked for you.'

Noticing Ranju"s disgruntled expression, she said, 'I'm not hearing any excuses today. Hurry up and get dressed and the driver will drop you.'

Ranju was left with no option but to obey her employer quietly. She sulked for a moment, but knew she had to do as she was told. In Ranju's absence, Jagdish brought Maya over to meet Mrs Banerjee who gave her an affectionate smile, and showered her with tenderness and warmth. Maya's almond-shaped, curious eyes and her friendly persona charmed everyone who met her. Mrs Banerjee was no different. She fell in love with her instantly. Maya was not only pretty, but also a charmer. She leapt forward to touch Mrs Banerjee's feet, who then cuddled Maya in her arms and sat her on her lap.

'Jagdish, please pass me the gift lying on the table. I've bought you a present and I hope you like it.'

Maya looked at her Barbie doll and said, 'Thank you, Aunty. I'll name her Rani.'

'Oh! That's a lovely name. She's adorable, Jagdish,' Mrs Banerjee's smiled.

Maya slipped off of Mrs Banerjee's lap, perched herself on a chair in the drawing room and settled down with her hamburger and Coke. Her chit-chat with Mrs Banerjee came to an end only when Rajan and Shalani Malhotra arrived twenty minutes later.

The Malhotras took to Maya like a moth to a flame,

and wanted to take her home with them without any delay. But Jagdish was reluctant. He had to prepare Maya for this change. He could not just push her into an unknown world. Besides, the long drawn out legal formalities had to be dealt with before Maya could be officially adopted. Rajan and Shalini had just one simple request—they did not want any links with Maya's past.

'As her mother is apathetic towards her and will easily sign her off at a later date, we would like to keep her with us till all the paperwork is completed,' requested Shalini. 'She is five years old and may well understand the fact that she is being adopted. Hence, we don't want to keep her from the truth.'

Maya's happiness and well-being was all that Jagdish and Gita wished for. They had helped Mamta in raising this child and felt a deep sense of duty towards her.

'Well then, it's settled. We'll let you know the venue and you can bring her along a week from today,' Rajan concluded.

Meanwhile, Shalini was engrossed in talking to Maya, who kept nodding her little head at everything she said. She sat close to her new mother and tightly held on to a bag of goodies she had brought for her. Shalini had her arm comfortably around Maya's shoulder, and there was a sparkle on her face which Rajan hadn't seen in a long time. She had discussed adopting a child with him several times. Now Maya was going to fill that void in their lives.

The night before Maya was to leave for her new home, Gita could not sleep and woke up Jagdish at four in the morning.

'My heart is restless and I can't get any sleep. How can we give Maya away and never see her again? Mamta was my best friend and I owe it to her. I will look after her,' she said, choking with despair.

Jagdish was gutted too, but he knew they had to be sensible. 'This is a golden opportunity for Maya to have a beautiful life. Knowing Mamta, I'm sure this is what she would want too.'

Gita was getting cold feet and wondered if Maya's new parents could give her the love and care she deserved. She was perturbed by negative thoughts and didn't want her little girl to go away.

'She will be fine,' Jagdish assured her. 'Besides, I can't take the financial burden of a child. I've just about finished settling our own children and soon we will be grandparents ourselves. I promise I'll ask Mrs Banerjee to let me know if she's unhappy and we can bring her back. Let's give it at least a chance. Besides, Maya is prepared to go and we must do what is good for her.'

He had told Maya, "Aunty and Uncle want you to stay with them. They were known to your grandmother and she liked them very much." He had to tell her a few white lies. Maya had no reason to be suspicious. She was a happy child and her Nani's vigilance, love and care had been a positive influence on her.

The Malhotras decided to pick up Maya at Taj Mahal

Hotel. Jagdish handed her over with a heavy heart. The Malhotras welcomed her with exuberance. A new chapter was about to unfold in Maya's life, as she was transported from her life in the slum to a world of comfort and luxury.

16

After seeing Maya for the first time, Shalini was thrilled at the prospect of being a mom. Her desire to welcome her daughter like a princess, decorate her room and give her the best the universe could offer, was palpable in the Malhotra household.

'The decorators are working round the clock and busy getting Maya's nursery ready. I wonder if there will be enough time for me to put in all the accessories tomorrow,' Shalini worried.

'Don't get stressed about this, Shalini. Maya's room will look beautiful when she walks in. I'm also very busy with the lawyer getting the paperwork sorted out as quickly as possible. I don't want to wait a single day longer than required to legally adopt our little bundle of joy.'

Rajan was anxious himself. 'You know how stringent adoption rules are. I want all the paperwork to be in order.' He had been sitting with his lawyers day and night, understanding the rules and regulations, not wanting to leave any loopholes.

'What is it that's so complicated?' Shalini was curious.

'People sometimes adopt for the wrong reasons, so

the government has to take precautions. Firstly we both have to be physically, mentally and emotionally stable, and financially capable. They want to be sure we are motivated enough to adopt a child and are free from any life-threatening medical conditions. Besides,' Rajan winked 'it's imperative for us to have been in a stable marital relationship for at least two years.'

Shalini nodded. 'It is cumbersome, but imagine… after all this time, we will finally have a child to share this house with.'

'Absolutely. Maya will have to be declared legally free by the child welfare committee and then the lawyers will register online for us with the Child Adoption Resource Information and Guidance System.' Rajan paused to catch his breath. He sat on the sofa and continued. It was important for Shalini to be aware too.

'The adoption agency in turn will prepare a home study report and the adoption petition will then be filed in court. The certified copy of the order will be obtained by the agency, and ten days after that we can call Maya our own.'

'Phew! Hurry, hurry Rajan. I can't wait.' Shalini's eyes lit up just at the thought of Maya soon being theirs.

Maya Malhotra's little fingers firmly held on to Shalini's sari as she walked out of Taj Hotel and into a completely new life. She turned around several times to look at Jagdish and wave, not understanding where she was going.

Afterwards, both Gita and Jagdish never spoke about Maya, but often cried when they were alone for weeks after Maya's departure. Ranju was relieved and happy. The Malhotra mansion at Malcha Marg was about three kilometres away from the slum, but that small distance became the most defining and significant journey of Maya's life. From her small, dilapidated shanty, Maya was transported to a surreal world of comfort and luxury.

It was a new beginning. Maya's life had changed forever.

As her swanky Jaguar cruised along, Maya's almond eyes curiously peeped out of the window. It was her maiden car ride and the experience was overwhelming. She had never really ventured out of her little shell in DID Colony. The rare outings with her Nani were restricted to shopping at Sarojini Nagar Market. Maya was spellbound by the beautiful gardens and opulent bungalows along the way.

'Would you like some cupcakes, my dear?' asked Shalini, trying to break the ice.

With a quaint smile and confused expression Maya instantly nodded her head.

Shalini had packed a little box of treats with marshmallows, cupcakes, cheese straws, candies and cream biscuits. Maya opened the box and picked out a handful of candies, the only familiar confectionery, and started munching. Shalini's eyes brimmed with tears.

As the car stopped at the red light Maya saw little kids selling roses and pens at the traffic signal. Their tattered clothes and unkempt hair painted a picture of complete neglect and misery. Only a day before, Maya herself had looked scruffy. Jagdish had bought her a new dress and Gita had combed back her hair in a ponytail before they had made their way to the Taj Hotel. She related to them, they were part of her world.

A little boy walked up to their car and extended his palm, begging for something to eat. His lean, fragile frame was barely covered by a torn t-shirt and his long, messy hair fell over his eyes. The agony and desperation in his voice was painted on his face. His pale hands firmly held an old mug for collecting change and with the other, he kept tapping the car window, his gaze firmly on the box of goodies kept on Maya's lap.

Maya looked at him and paused, waiting for her mother to give her a cue. But Shalini smiled at her without reading her mind.

'Can I give him some candies?' Maya asked her mother hesitantly.

'Of course you can, my darling,' replied Shalini, readily pulling down the window.

Extending her hand out of the window she gave the boy a cupcake.

'Aunty, you are like my Nani. She always carried a packet of sweets and distributed it to the children on the road.'

'You must call me Mummy, okay? And that is your Papa.'

Maya was somewhat disturbed by this, and suddenly

the happy child turned despondent. Tears rolled down her cheeks. The word 'mummy' only had frightful memories attached to it. Shalini slid towards her and took her in her arms. Life had been harsh and ruthless for this little soul. But now, all that was behind her.

As the watchman opened the gates to their palatial bungalow, Maya eyes lit up with sheer delight. Her new parents had made elaborate arrangements to welcome her home. The driveway was beautifully decorated with mauve and pink coloured balloons. The meticulously trimmed hedges were resplendent with strings of twinkling fairy lights. To celebrate the homecoming of their beautiful, little angel into their fold, the Malhotras had organised a lavish feast for all their workers and their families.

It was a stupendous new world: a life that Maya had never dreamt of. Her life so far had been around clustered huts, narrow by-lanes, open drains and the blaring sounds of DID Colony. The Malhotra mansion on the other hand was a treat to the senses: beautifully manicured gardens lined with gulmohar trees, shrubs of white bougainvillea, bloody lily, African moon, alpinia and calatheas; the plush home decor and furniture which had been hand-picked and imported from their trips abroad; the soft sound of piano notes playing in the background and of course, the artwork that adorned the walls. The special editions of Lalique and Baccarat placed on the glass shelves were a sight to behold. Everything she saw and experienced was the epitome of opulence and grandeur. Shalini even had miniature bonsai plants, which she personally supervised, in her den.

Shalini was the embodiment of grace and elegance. She dressed in gorgeous chiffon saris, with her hair always blow-dried at the hair dressers'. Her big, black eyes were like a window into her compassionate soul. Every morning, as Rajan sat in the garden sipping tea and flipping through newspapers, Shalini would feed the sparrows and pigeons that hovered around for their breakfast.

Rajan was an industrialist and and a philanthropist, owning two pharmaceutical-manufacturing factories. He was a tall man with an athletic physique. His knowledge, wit and impressive personality made him a darling among his friends, colleagues and relatives. His love to entertain compelled Shalani to throw parties virtually every other day. He had a passion for food and he occupied the kitchen on Sundays with their cook. He had travelled the world extensively.

For Maya, the material comforts were secondary. She would now come to have the one thing she had always craved—the love and security of parents. Shalini and Rajan embraced her wholeheartedly. There was an instant connect between Maya and Shalini. Today, as they walked into their home hand in hand, Maya had never felt so special. Although Mamta and Gita had unconditionally loved her and mothered her, Maya had craved her mother's affection. Her strained relationship with Ranju had left a deep, indelible scar on her soul.

Drawing her closer, Shalini kissed her forehead and said, 'Let's go to your room, darling, so that you can freshen up and relax before the party.'

Maya quickly tightened her grip around Shalini's little finger and followed her up the stairs. As Shalini turned the knob and opened the room, Maya was enraptured by a magical land of fairy tales.

The evening sun filtering through the glass windows illuminated every corner of the room. The walls were painted pastel peach and pink, while the windowsills were adorned with little plants. A toy cabinet standing next to the bed was filled with dolls, toys, picture books, puzzles and PlayStations. However, one thing that instantly caught Maya's fancy was a beautiful, hand-painted bird feeder hanging in the balcony. As a little sparrow stopped by for water, Maya quickly ran to the window and stood behind the curtains, silently admiring the bird's antics.

On this special day, the Malhotras' house was bustling with activity. Prakash, the chief caretaker and butler of the mansion, was dictating orders and supervising the arrangements. Rajan and Shalini had preferred a novel way of sharing their joy and celebrating Maya's arrival. Instead of a clichéd social affair, they had invited the families of all their staff and children from the nearby NDMC School. There was an enormous spread of mouth-watering delicacies, from traditional Bengali desserts like rosogulla and mishti doi to Punjabi favourites like samosa and chaat, along with Gujarati numbers like khandvi and dhokla. For the kids, Shalini had curated small gift bags filled with colouring books, crayons, candies and story books.

As the clock struck four, guests began assembling in

their garden and Shalini scurried upstairs to get Maya ready for the party. The fancy bathtub had replaced the iron bucket which her Nani had to get in line to fill every day for Maya's bath. There were bottles of cream, shampoo and shower gel neatly placed on a glass shelf. Maya felt like a fairy lost in wonderland. Shalini dressed her in a purple, polka-dotted, knee-length frock and white bellies. Tucked in one corner of her closet was a small treasure chest of beautiful little trinkets: hair clips, bracelets, strings of pearls, silver brooches and Maya's favourite accessory—bangles. She stared down at them for a second and then impulsively hauled them out of the drawer. As a solitary tear escaped from the corner of her eye, memories of her Nani flashed though her mind. How she loved going with her to Sarojini Nagar during Diwali to buy new glass bangles every year. Shalini sensed Maya's melancholy.

'You look beautiful, my girl. Let's go downstairs now. I think it's a good time for some ice cream.'

As mother and daughter walked hand in hand towards the dining hall, Rajan silently stood by the door and admired the bond between them. The celebrations continued for hours and the Malhotras proudly introduced their daughter to all their visitors. Maya Malhotra had started her new journey.

17

Rajan and Shalini were the ideal couple. They backed each other's aspirations and were achievers in their own right. They were well-educated, sensible, compassionate and liberal. Maya had added a new dimension to their lives. Despite his busy work schedule, Rajan made time for family picnics and bedtime storytelling sessions. Maya was an affable, obedient and well-mannered child. With boundless affection and care, Rajan and Shalini were optimistic she would grow into a stellar young lady. Although Shalini was a hands-on mom, she had a trail of domestic helpers and maids to help her at all times.

It had been two weeks since Maya had walked into the Malhotra household. She had now settled down in her new environment. On a bright Sunday morning, as the family sat down to enjoy a scrumptious breakfast, Rajan gave them a surprise.

'I have booked tickets for the latest Disney movie at PVR.'

Maya looked dazed. She hadn't heard of Disney or movie halls, and had no clue what her father was talking about. Micky Mouse, Bugs Bunny, Donald Duck, Scrooge McDuck and Launchpad McQuack were not woven into her life as a child.

Shalini brought out her picture books 'Look at these characters. Many of them you'll see in the movie. I'll get some videos too, so you can start to recognize the other characters. What about some stuffed toys? Aww, you'll love Mickey Mouse beta'.

Maya jumped off the chair, ran towards Rajan and hugged him.

'What about me Maya darling?' Shalini could not resist teasing Maya. She looked at her mother shyly and moved forward with open arms.

That afternoon, while driving towards the movie theatre, Maya could barely contain her curiosity. She persistently asked questions and Shalini happily answered each one of them. Watching a movie in a cinema hall, eating a tub of caramel and cheese popcorn with a Coke was an amazing experience, a luxury Maya couldn't have dreamt of.

As they drove past Gymkhana Club, Rajan received an urgent call from his office and pulled over. Waiting in the car, Maya suddenly spotted Ranju in the far distance. It was two in the afternoon and she was probably visiting Gita aunty, carrying a bag of vegetables. For a moment Maya was stunned. She couldn't decipher the complex emotions tugging at her heartstrings. She had dearly missed her Nani's affectionate hugs and the unconditional love of Gita aunty and Jagdish uncle. But Ranju's apathy had constructed a barrier which spawned soreness in her little mind. Perplexed and dewy-eyed, she looked away and coiled into her seat, trying to hide the agony of the yesteryears from the world. It seemed difficult to repair the feeling of being unwanted, which was ingrained deep in her heart. She was too shy to point her real mother out to her new parents.

It took Rajan and Shalini a few months to enrol Maya into one of the top schools of Delhi, and thus began a defining new chapter in her life. The crisp, new uniform, school bag and fancy water bottle were incentives to get her ready for her first day at school. Maya evinced a keen interest in books. For hours, she would sit in Rajan's library, flipping through the pages of her picture and story books, trying to imitate her father. Her parents also fuelled her interest in art and her writing desk was stacked with a series of different encyclopaedias. Her drawers were bursting with jewellery-making kits and play-dough. With a small spade and shovel, she would regularly accompany her mother to the garden and help her plant saplings. Maya was never denied a thing; in fact, she was spoiled with excessive gifts. Family vacations every other weekend were her treasured time; she loved being with her parents. Maya also looked forward to Sundays when her father was at home and also devouring Shalini's delectable meals. The day would be spent in harmony: reading books, watching cartoons and playing board games.

'I must say, it's only a year and Maya has gained confidence and grace beyond recognition,' a surprised Shalini proudly told Rajan.

'Indeed, it's all your hard work and her eagerness to learn, my dear,' replied an upbeat Rajan.

For a six-year-old Maya was mature and judicious. On the surface, she didn't come across as a perturbed child, but she had trouble conquering the agony of her childhood. Memories of her life at DID Colony and her complex relationship with her mother haunted her.

At school, Maya remained aloof and struggled to make friends. She was awkward in spite of being a bright student and the encouraging teachers. She could not acknowledge that she was an adopted child. While Rajan and Shalini loved her without a doubt, they failed to see the emotional turmoil brewing in her heart. There were nights when she would wake up restless and sit at her desk early in the morning, even before Shalini came to wake her up. Sometimes, the Lego sets and Barbie dolls failed to interest her and she yearned for her Nani—her lap, her kisses and her cuddles.

One Year Later

It was a foggy Monday morning in January. Maya had reached school early that day. While waiting for the morning assembly to begin, she sat down on the stairs leading to the hallway and immersed herself in the new story book her mother had gifted her. Books not only kindled her interest, but also acted as a shield from the outside world. A tap on her shoulder made her look up in surprise.

'Hi! My name is Avika,' said the little girl, smiling from ear to ear.

Her effervescent voice and big, bright eyes were infectious. Maya gave her a hearty handshake.

'I am so glad that I'm not the only one to arrive so early. We still have fifteen minutes to go before the morning assembly begins. Do you want to come for a walk? I can show you a secret hideout that we discovered yesterday,' said Avika.

Maya welcomed Avika's idea. As they walked hand in hand through the corridors and gardens, the giggles became louder. Maya was happy to find a new friend. Over the next few weeks, they became close friends and spent most of their free time together. They shared many common interests like reading and painting, but in contrast to Maya's reserved demeanour, Avika was boisterous and unrestrained. Her house was less than a mile away from Maya's and they regularly started to visit the colony park together. The evenings were spent playing in Maya's doll house and riding tricycles.

Besides being a diligent student, Rajan discovered Maya's inclination towards sports and enrolled her in a tennis academy. Summer afternoons were spent swimming in Gymkhana Club and tennis practice. After a few months of training, Maya showed potential to become a fine tennis player and was selected for the club's junior doubles team. Shalini and Rajan were proud parents.

Rajan had expanded his overseas business and travelled a great deal. To atone for his absence, he overindulged Maya with presents.

'You are spoiling her with gifts, Rajan,' Shalini often complained. 'I understand that you love her immensely, but children must learn to appreciate the worth of every penny.'

But Rajan ignored Shalini's concerns and never failed to surprise Maya with expensive gifts. One evening he brought home an electric two-seater car and spent two hours teaching her to drive it. Her branded clothes were on par with Hollywood celebrity kids, and her little vanity case often amused Shalini. Maya would stand in front of the mirror and mess up her face. Then look at her mother for an approval.

'She's too little, for God's sake, Rajan.' But Rajan would indulge his wife with an affectionate kiss and pamper her too. Shalini learnt to shrug her shoulders and leave father and daughter alone. Rajan didn't know any other way to show his love.

Over the next five years with the Malhotras, Maya's life went from strength to strength and her future was as bright as it could be. But in spite of having everything her parents offered, she still couldn't let go of the darkness of her past. She nursed the pain, the indifference of her mother and clung to it like ivy.

At eleven, Maya entered her pre-teens and there was a growing streak of rebellion in her. Like most kids her age, she had to follow her peers and create a unique identity for herself. Her impatience to be popular and confident like Avika often pushed her to emulate her. Avika was not only bright, she was also a trained Kathak dancer. During cultural programmes and extra-curricular competitions, Avika would lead her team and win laurels for the school. Maya was competitive and envious of her occasionally.

'I want to look better than Avika at Payal's birthday party,' she said one day, while her mother was braiding her hair.

After a pause Shalini said, 'It's not a competition, my dear! You both look gorgeous. Never compare yourself to others, you are unique and have your own gifts. Never worry about what other people think. Beta, life isn't a race.' Shalini didn't fancy her daughter growing up into a jealous, envious adult.

But the faultlines had begun to appear. Maya would often snap at the smallest discords and never missed an opportunity to denigrate Avika. Sadly, she was unable to direct her talent productively. Rajan and Shalini were extremely disturbed by Maya's attitude.

'I really can't understand what's happening to Maya?' Shalini shared her concern with Rajan.

'I am to blame. Maybe it's the endless pampering that has spoilt her'.

'Don't blame yourself. I started to observe her more closely. She has mood swings and sometimes, she sits in your library and broods.'

'What about her academic performance?

'Well that's deteriorated too. She spends virtually all her time alone. If I join her she gets irritable and makes an excuse to go to her room.'

Rajan and Shalini were at their wit's end, not knowing how to handle her.

She loved sketching and painting, and through her love of art, she expressed her hidden perplexities. As she grew older, she had vivid dreams of her childhood, lighting up her sorrow. Every once in a while she'd wake up startled, like someone was trying to stifle her with a pillow. When she passed by the road leading to DID Colony she turned her face away. Questions she never understood as a child now nagged at her consciously, adding to her pre-teen problems.

One evening, while returning from her tennis class, Maya was stuck in a dreadful traffic jam. The roads were blocked for VIP movement and the area was thrown into complete chaos. Her driver's resolve to beat the traffic to get Maya home in time for her maths tuition led him to take a shortcut through DID Colony. The ice-cream vendor standing at the crossroads, the clustered shanties, and people sitting outside their homes seemed like a postcard from her past.

As the car moved slowly, Maya saw the neem tree, her eyes frantically searching for a glimpse of Gita aunty and Jagdish uncle, bringing back poignant memories of her childhood. A chill ran down her spine.

Sitting in her BMW, Maya saw the stark contrast between her past and present life. As a little kid she had seen her Nani toil all day to provide them food, and her new family spent a fortune on just toiletries. Nothing had changed in her birthplace. Just for a moment, she wished to step out of the car and walk through those narrow alleys once again, run into Gita aunty's arms and embrace her. The smell of freshly fried samosas at the tea stall brought flashbacks of evening strolls with her Nani. The slum was decorated with colourful banners, gold streamers and lights: there was euphoria all around. A crowd of people were dressed in bright, traditional attire. A wedding function seemed to be underway. Just as the car turned the corner, Maya saw a familiar face scrambling towards the crowd. Maya turned cold when she saw her biological mother.

You are still in your pitiable state. You are being taught a lesson for treating me so shabbily, her little mind thought with resentment.

Ranju went to a group of women and joined their friendly banter. She was dressed in an orange sari and her long braid was adorned with a string of mogra flowers. She looked lean and weak, but her smiling face expressed a pleasant equanimity. Maya cast her mind back to the day when Ranju had signed the adoption papers in the courtroom, and mercilessly pushed her towards the Malhotras. While Gita and Jagdish had cried inconsolably, Ranju had grunted, pulled a face and marched off. Maya's eyes had followed her, her little mind unable to understand. Being elbowed while she sat by her Nani's dead body, being suffocated by a pillow, being unloved and hated, had left an indelible scar in her heart and mind.

Maya had not understood it then, but the feeling of abandonment had stayed with her. As she grew older things fell into perspective and hurt and pain buried itself in a corner of her heart.

She could not bury the echoes of past conversations between Gita aunty and her Nani, criticizing Ranju's apathy for her child. She was unable to forgive her mother. She sat back in her seat and closed her eyes. As the car rolled up the driveway at the Malhotra mansion, Maya stepped out and ran up the stairs straight to her room. She felt emotionally choked and the canvas became her best friend that night. With brushstrokes and smeared fingers she poured her heart out, till the morning sun rose to dispel the darkness.

It was the month of November and the landscape had donned its winter coat. The sun gleamed weakly through the foggy and chilly mornings. Delhi was at its glorious best before the biting cold. In the last few weeks, the Malhotra family had been constantly busy. Each one was absorbed with their own activities. Maya had been moody over the past few days, hence one morning, Rajan and Shalini had decided to accompany their daughter to school. Sitting with Maya in the back seat of the car, Shalini held her hand and kissed her forehead.

'So how is my little angel this morning', she said, peering intensely into her eyes. 'If there is anything that bothers you, feel free to share it with us,' said Shalini.

'Shalini, she's no longer little. She's going to turn fifteen very soon,' Rajan intervened, trying to initiate a light-hearted conversation. 'Let's plan our annual holiday around your special day. How about an African safari? We have been thinking about it for quite some time now. I can take five days off from work and we can go.'

'Wow, Papa, I'd love that! I studied the tribes of Maasai Mara and have watched the wildebeest migration across the Serengeti on TV,' Maya was ecstatic. Avika has never been on a safari.'

'You must take a lot of photographs too and show them to your friends. In fact, I'll take videos and then you can invite your buddies home to watch it,' Shalini piped in.

'Thank you so much, Papa! What a fantastic fifteenth birthday present. Mummy we have so much to prepare.'

Shalini and Rajan laughed, exchanging a glance of relief.

Over the next week, Rajan planned the perfect holiday itinerary. 'It would be exhilarating just to watch the animals in their natural habitat. I've ordered a new camera with a powerful zoom lens. I want our photos to be perfect.'

'Papa, what a cool idea! Mummy and I are going to spend our evenings shopping for safari clothes. We'll also surf the internet and make a long list of 'must do' things in Kenya.'

'This evening after your Maths tuition we can browse around South Ex and see what's available,' Shalini said, as enthusiastic as her daughter.

'Can I miss tuition today, please Mummy?' Maya asked her mother in a baby voice.

Shalini raised her eyebrows and shook her head firmly. Maya looked at her father. He smiled and pointed his finger to his wife. Shalini nodded a firm no again.

It was a splendid time to visit the Mara, as it marked the dry season in the southern African continent.

In Kenya, Rajan had arranged a wonderful surprise for Maya's special day. Before sunrise, the Malhotras headed five miles north for an intoxicating ride in a hot air balloon. The trip had clearly brought back some life in Maya and she couldn't quell her excitement for days after she returned to school.

On the other hand, for Gita and Jagdish, Maya's birthday was ushered with sad memories of her and Mamta. They had had no news of her since the day Ranju had officially signed the adoption papers. Jagdish often asked Mrs Banerjee about her wellbeing, but she politely refused to divulge any information. Mrs Banerjee stuck to her word. She had promised Rajan and Shalini to never disclose the details of Maya's new life. It was important to keep her past life separate from the present.

18

With each passing year Maya was growing up to be a beautiful young lady, but Rajan's indulgence made her impudent and reckless. She had a chauffeur-driven car, a credit card for expenses, the latest gadgets and the best designer clothes. Maya hid her insecurities behind the ostentations of wealth. Her opulent lifestyle attracted a lot of attention at school as well. At seventeen, when most of her classmates were planning and preparing for college, Maya was completely clueless She would spend hours in front of a canvas, giving vent to the revolts within her. Painting, her true companion, would ease her anguish. The dreary colours often evoked questions in Shalini's mind. Was Maya still holding on to her past and struggling with her daunting childhood? Or was there some other issue? Why were the colours in her paintings always so dreary? Was something troubling her? Maya kept her turbulence close to her chest, and built barriers, even with her mother, on the subjects of her past.

On the night before Diwali, Maya took Rajan's permission for a sleepover party at Shreya's place. Shreya was her doubles partner in the school tennis team, and the two had lately established a new equation and spent a lot of time together. Avika suspected that Shreya's company had a negative influence on Maya's behaviour. They often bunked school and spent time in trivial gossip. With Shreya and her friends, Maya felt a sense of deliverance. There were no rules, no inhibitions and no boundaries. She enjoyed the popularity and attention, but failed to recognize that she was being used as an ATM. She would generously buy them gifts, take them out for fancy treats and pay their bills. Avika tried to counsel her, but her advice fell on deaf ears.

For the pre-Diwali celebration, Maya was dressed up in a Rohit Bal gown. The party commenced at seven pm. As their friends streamed in, the music got louder and the girls hit the dance floor. Maya had offered to pay for the dinner, which she had ordered from Moti Mahal. When the doorbell rang Maya went to open it and was startled to see Abhay and his friends outside.

Abhay was the sports captain of their school and Shreya's neighbour. His family had shifted from Wisconsin in the US to Delhi two years ago. Abhay was tall and lean with an athletic physique. His dark, brown eyes, chiselled jawline and baritone voice had a bevy of girls fawning over him. He was vain and knew the girls swooned over his hunky good looks. He sang and played the guitar and was undoubtedly the life of a party. He was charming with an enigmatic charisma and affable personality.

'Come in boys! We have been waiting for you,' Shreya said, as she took Abhay's hand and pulled him in. Maya hadn't a clue he had been invited. She had a secret crush on him, and here he was acknowledging her with a smile. As Abhay came forward and extended his hand towards Maya, her heart skipped a beat.

'Hi! Glad to see you. Wow, how beautiful you look all dressed up! For a minute I didn't recognize you,' he said, while Maya smiled coyly and shook his hand.

Abhay's charm enhanced her adulation to heights she had never known before. The party continued till the wee hours of the morning and the drinks, brought by the boys, flowed freely. Maya kept stealing glances at Abhay sitting across the room. She was too shy to approach him, but was jealous as he danced with the other girls, casually flirting with each one. After most of the guests left, Shreya and her band of friends huddled around a bonfire in the backyard. The giggles and chatter echoed through the thick winter fog. From hilarious anecdotes to childhood memories and ghost encounters, the stories pursued till the night turned the corner to enter another beautiful part of the world. With the approaching orange glow of the rising sun Maya made a resolve to buy her way into a group where her complexes didn't intimidate her. She felt liberated from the protective vigil of her parents; far away from all rules and regulations. She remained strictly reticent about her early life; she was never going to open up a chapter which would leave her ashamed in front of her friends.

'Should I get you something to drink?' Abhay asked with a glint in his eyes, trying to engage with her. He extended the bottle of beer which he was drinking.

Maya's face lit up with delight. She nodded, moved quickly away from her friends and pushed his hand away, gently taking a step towards the dining room. Abhay followed, putting his arm around her shoulder. Maya, although a teetotaller, had to keep up with her crush. She guzzled two beers without thinking. Her head did swoon that night as she sat on the beanbag by the window, and listened to Abhay rattle on about his interests, aspirations, favourite movies and music. They shared a lot in common, including their love for sports and travelling. As the winter breeze gushed through the window and the wind chimes sang in unison, Maya and Abhay found warmth in each other's arms. Holding her gently by the waist, Abhay pulled her closer and kissed her lips tenderly. Maya succumbed to his charms. She had never had any romantic encounter before, but Abhay was certainly her Romeo.

Thus ensued a new chapter in Maya's life. She met Abhay after school and hung out together, with their friends in tow. The Gymkhana Club was their favourite place where they often played tennis together. Rajan and Shalini also liked Abhay. They knew his parents socially, and were amazed by his confidence and maturity. They felt he was a good influence on Maya and welcomed him home. Abhay became an anchor for Maya's troubled heart. For so many years, she had grappled with her own identity and insecurities. Now, she felt sure of herself. In a short span of three months, Maya developed a strong emotional bond with Abhay.

He would entertain her with his humorous antics and witty retorts. They would watch movies and play video games on her PlayStation when he wasn't busy. Abhay was a talented soccer player and was keen to pursue the sport professionally. He had even applied to a prestigious soccer academy in Los Angeles. His zeal and commitment towards his goal was unparalleled. He constantly coaxed Maya to apply for college to universities abroad and often said, 'You must be more focussed about your future plans, Maya. There is a sea of opportunities out there. This is our time to shine and prove our abilities. If you want to become an artist then seriously think of joining an art school and pursuing what you love most.'

'I haven't decided yet. I love painting but let's see what I want to do. My parents have no issues if I apply to any art school round the world. They think I'm good.'

'Then why don't you? Applications and admissions take months.'

Maya, totally disinterested in pursuing this conversation, quickly jumped to tennis.

'I was thinking of inviting Shreya for a doubles game tomorrow. Why don't you ask a friend?'

Abhay was no fool. 'Honestly Maya, get serious or you'll end up being a parasite on your dad.'

Unfazed, Maya looked him in the eye, 'Stop being like a nagging wife. I'll decide soon enough. Even my parents don't hammer me with this topic all the time.' Abhay had no choice but to back off.

Abhay's presence had nourished the void in Maya's life, and she valued nothing more than just being around him even at the cost of completely losing sight of her own priorities and ambition. She became extremely possessive and vulnerable. She was intolerant when Abhay spoke to other girls. Their petty fights often left Abhay infuriated.

Although summer was at its peak, the Malhotras had no summer plans. Rajan had business associates visiting from abroad, and getting away from Delhi was not possible. He had committed to visiting Mumbai with his collaborators. Maya was happy to stay back and enjoy her summer holidays with Abhay. One day, while waiting for him at the Gymkhana Club cafe, sipping on her favourite ginger ice tea, she saw Abhay rushing towards her.

'There's some good news, Maya!' he exclaimed. 'I just received a mail from the sports academy in Los Angeles. If everything falls in place, I will be flying to the United States by the end of July.'

Maya just sat on the sofa with a blank expression. The thought of living away from Abhay was unbearable. She did not congratulate him or share her sadness.

The next few weeks were marked by several arguments and sleepless nights. Maya didn't want him to travel, but Abhay was single-minded about pursuing his dream. No one in the world could compel him to give it up.

The disagreements and altercations between them soon became acrimonious. Maya's perfect little fairytale was ripped apart and she was unable to take control of the situation or her feelings.

The day soon arrived for Abhay to leave. He had a two-year training programme and had planned to complete his studies simultaneously. He called Maya several times and tried talking to her, but she refused. She found solace in the company of her friend Shreya and her gang. She would sleep over at her place, pretending to study, while partying till the wee hours every other day. Bunking classes, missing assignments and other nefarious activities made their group infamous in school.

One evening, as the overcast sky thundered in absolute glory, Maya sat down by the window and reminisced about the wonderful times she shared with Abhay. The raindrops trickling down the window pane seemed to mirror the tears streaming down her cheeks. A knock on the door suddenly shattered her reverie and she hurriedly wiped away her tears. Shalini had invited Shreya for dinner and a sleepover that night. She had prepared a huge delectable spread of appetizers, salads and Maya's favourite Italian food. She just wanted Maya to be happy again.

'I have a little surprise for you, my darling,' Shreya whispered into Maya's ear as soon as Shalini left the room.

Maya eagerly began searching Shreya's handbag for her surprise gift. With much care and precision, she began to transfer the clutter of Shreya's bag on to the study table.

'I have it right here in my pocket,' said Shreya, pulling out a small pouch from her zipper. With a mischievous glint in her eyes, she rushed to the door and locked it from inside.

'What are you doing?' asked Maya.

'Magic! You just have to trust me. I will take you to heaven.'

From that little pouch of 'magic', Shreya pulled out some green stems and a thin sheet of paper.

'Do you have a lighter?' she asked as Maya looked at her in utter disbelief.

Shreya crushed some of the leaves, removed the seeds, rolled it into a cigarette.

'Do you want a taste of euphoria?' Shreya asked, as she lit up the joint and took a long drag.

'Are you serious? What the hell are you smoking?' asked Maya.

'Marijuana.'

Maya was speechless. She had seen a few of Abhay's friends smoking weed, but had never tried it herself.

'Try it once,' Shreya insisted. 'You can thank me later.'

Maya was hesitant and confused. Her heart and mind were tangled up. That night, her sense of judgement was overpowered by curiosity. The first drag was a little harsh and made her cough. But fifteen minutes later, Maya was buoyant and relaxed. This *was* magic. It helped her forget her anxiety and heartache. The colours became more vivid and the music became louder. The heightened sensory perception was accompanied by an enhanced ability to concentrate. Maya felt lazy and lost, tired and hungry at the same time. Everything seemed more beautiful, more dramatic. It was a surreal world and she loved it. She wanted to run away from the chaos. She wanted to break free and fly away.

Over the next few weeks and months, marijuana became Maya's constant companion for the sleepless nights. Before she could take stock of the situation, the smoke had completely engulfed her life. Dependency on any stimulating substance was a worrying sign, especially for a teenager. Rajan and Shalini were perturbed by Maya's behaviour. Her mercurial mood swings had worsened and poor academic performance were a matter of concern. Her twelfth board exams were a year away and she had to focus. Her untidy room and life were a reflection of the chaos brewing within her. Her traumatic childhood, failed teenage romance and substance abuse became the perfect recipe for her to go down the tube. She took her life at home for granted.

'Where did we go wrong, Rajan?' Shalini would often ask and break down into tears.

'Our unequivocal love and pampering, Maya is still forlorn…

'Spend time with her in her room or coax her to come and sit in the garden for some fresh air when you are helping the gardener. Take her out shopping, for movies or an occasional spa visit. Maybe she needs some distraction after Abhay.'

Rajan also consciously took time out from his work

schedule and tried to nourish the bond between father and daughter. Family dinners, morning walks, weekend getaways—he did all he could. The Malhotras were anxious to go the extra mile in order to bring back Maya's effervescent smile.

'What is the matter, darling? Why are you playing with your food? Can I pass you something?' Shalini often asked when the family sat down for dinner.

'I'm doing good, mummy. Not hungry at all.'

'You didn't even eat your lunch properly, beta.'

'Why are you over fussing all the time? When I'm hungry, I'll eat.'

'Behave yourself, Maya, and don't take that tone with your mother,' Rajan would be forced to intervene.

Maya would irritably push her chair back and storm off in a huff.

'Come back immediately, Maya!'

'I can't understand what's wrong with her? She's not eating, she's losing weight and looking emaciated,' Shalini would turn to Rajan for support.

'She's in her teens and children go through strange phases. Don't push her too hard or she'll become defiant. Just follow her closely and try and find out if something is wrong or if she's just a normal rebellious teenager.'

'I've known Maya to be moody, but this is another level.'

'Yes, I agree.'

'Do you think I should go to school tomorrow and speak to her class teacher?'

'No, leave it for now. She'll get hyper and things will get worse,' Rajan tried to placate Shalini.

'Is she painting at all?' he gently changed the topic.

'No, she sits in front of the canvas for hours but doesn't paint,' Shalini pushed her chair back. 'I'll go check on her.'

A week later, while sorting out Maya's wardrobe, Shalini chanced upon her stash of weed, carefully hidden beneath a pile of magazines. She was shocked. As if all those years of love and care had suddenly dissipated into thin air. It was imperative to talk to Maya.

'Where did we go wrong, Rajan? Did we neglect her? I, as a mother, did my best,' Shalini cried all night as she lay in Rajan's arms.

'Don't be so harsh on yourself. We both know Maya had a disturbed childhood and maybe we ignored the fact that she still had issues which she hadn't worked through. These things can be related to peer pressure at school or even Abhay. Come here Shalini, we'll resolve this together.'

After much deliberation, they both finally decided to seek professional counselling. Now, the main task was gaining Maya's confidence to trust their course of action, without her becoming unnerved. Rajan sat her down in his study as Shalini stood by the sofa to one side.

'Beta, mummy found some weed in your cupboard four days ago.'

Maya sat up to full attention.

'Don't say a word, Maya. No need for a knee-jerk reaction. Just absorb what I'm saying and think it through calmly. Mummy and I will wait for your reply after two days.'

Maya bit her lip, blinked and looked away. She fidgeted with her fingers, a childhood habit she had inherited from her mother and rose from the chair, too antsy to sit still in this turmoil. She left the room without a word.

Initially, Maya was a little apprehensive and reluctant to discuss her dilemma with her parents, but finally she capitulated. Her constant worries had to be unloaded before she could grow as a person again, which she wanted. Her inclination to identify how she intended to shape her future was important. Yes, she needed help. Who could be better than her parents to help her through this tough phase?

A day later Maya knocked on her parents' bedroom door early in the morning and poured her heart out. She lay between them and acknowledged her angst, her dread and her complexes. Her lips trembled as the guilt flowed over her face.

'We love you more than anyone in the whole wide world. Don't punish yourself because of who you are. Many children are adopted or grow up with problems. They can be financial, domestic abuse or something else. There's nothing to be ashamed of. Each one of us is born with our destiny, how we handle what has been doled out to us is important. You are your own person and will be known for the future you carve out for yourself. A broken relation cannot dampen your spirits to an extent that you become your own enemy. An intelligent and talented girl like you can do wonders with your life,' Rajan assured her.

'We are your parents and that's all there is to it. Your biological mother was uneducated and didn't know better.'

Maya did not know what had happened to her mother. Shalini and Rajan were not going to open up a pandora's box. She was young and emotionally vulnerable, giving her such sensitive information was pointless. It was imperative to get their daughter back on track.

Maya listened in silence, holding on to her parents' hands.

'Don't close yourself, Maya. Be brave and talk to us freely, we will do whatever we can to pull you out of this. We are not angry and we want to help.'

Rajan and Shalini had decided to take a soft approach and build up her trust for them now and in the future.

'Don't worry about anything, darling. We understand how you must feel at times. But we are always there for you. Never hesitate to communicate with us,' Shalini put a comforting arm around her.

Maya lay quietly for a few minutes and then slowly crawled out of their bed. She stood by the edge staring at both of them with a smile on her face, and tears rolling down her cheeks. Slowly she walked out of their room. Shalini sat up to follow Maya, but Rajan stopped her.

'Give her some space.'

Shalini sank back on her pillow, hoping this dreadful phase would soon pass.

A recovery programme was worked out. Not everything about her life had to be changed but a few things and new behaviours had to be introduced, which would help her stay out of trouble. Shalini got an art teacher to come home after school, so she would be busy doing what she loved most—painting. Shalini made sure that a friend, a neighbour or her favourite aunty and uncle were over for dinner often. She had to eat well and gain some weight. At nights, Shalini slept in Maya's room while she studied for her board exams. It didn't matter to her parents if she didn't pass the exam with flying colours. A healthy, happy child was all they wanted. It was crucial to keep her relaxed and busy. Above everything, it was important for Maya to be honest with herself, which she was. She reached out to her parents when she had bad days and craved for inner peace. She studied through the nights, till Shalini had to pull her away from her desk.

'I want you and Papa to be proud of me, mummy. I have it all and I was foolishly going to throw it all away. I'm so sorry for putting you and Papa through so much anguish.'

'Our doll is a brave, sensible girl, Papa and I both have no doubts about that,' Shalini kissed her forehead.

After a few months of therapy and counselling, Maya soon regained her confidence and managed to fight her inner demons. Rajan and Shalini monitored her activities and guided her wisely. They had been oblivious about when they had crossed the thin line between love and overindulgence. They often failed to remember that she had been adopted when she was five years old and had memories. They could not talk her through the mystery of who she really was and where she came from. With a little tolerance, patience and support, they managed to mend the damage. Even Avika stood by her friend, giving her much-needed encouragement and support. Never did she make her feel inadequate in any way. Maya started spending more time with her family, appreciating Avika like never before. She channelized her energy productively and soon regained her faith in herself.

The time had come for Maya to chart her journey for the future. She was a proficient artist, a competent tennis player and well read too. Her love for reading had led her to a wide array of subjects, cultures and philosophies. Maya had developed a keen interest in studying law, specifically human rights. A close friend and associate of Rajan owned a law consulting firm in Mumbai. During one of his visits to the capital, Maya had had the opportunity to learn and discuss the possibilities of a career in law with him,. He was extremely encouraging and helpful. He not only suggested a few good books to read after her exams, but also helped shortlist some prestigious law schools. With new dreams and aspirations, Maya was once again moving towards a new horizon, leaving behind the emotional baggage of the yesteryear.

After much research and contemplation, Maya sat with her father in his library and discussed her future.

'I've decided to apply for a bachelor's in law at the Trinity College, Papa. It is a four-year programme, offering a dual degree in law and political science. It is a high-ranking, reputed university, with good career prospects for the future. What's your view, Papa?

'If that's what you are passionate about, then that's what you must do. I'm specifically impressed by the work of institutions who are working against human rights abuse. If you plan to specialize in the field of human rights laws, it will hone your knowledge and skills for the service of society. Law must be accessible to all, and not just the privileged few.'

'I'm happy you approve of my decision. I discussed many options with Mummy and eventually zeroed in on law. She said to discuss it with you and take help in the applications. Now that it's all decided, Papa, let's celebrate.'

'Done! You decide the venue and be ready at nine pm. Ask Avika, if you like.'

Sitting in her balcony, away from all the commotion in the Malhotra mansion over the food parcels that had to be packed for her travel, she was going through a gamut of emotions. As she reminisced about her childhood days—the Sunday brunches, bedtime stories, beach vacations, birthday parties and innumerable moments of unadulterated joy—she silently thanked her parents for giving her the love and opportunity of being who she was today. Her eyes sparkled with eager anticipation for her future in Dublin.

19

Along with her bags, Rajan and Shalini had packed a plethora of love and blessings for their darling daughter. Dropping her off at the airport, Rajan hugged her tightly and kissed her forehead, as Shalini stood there, holding back her tears.

'We are extremely proud of you, Maya,' Rajan said as he handed her a sealed envelope. 'You have a long journey ahead of you and this is the beginning of a new milestone. Focus on your degree and we will see you once you have settled down. I'm so proud you're going to Dublin, all by yourself. My little girl is all grown up now.'

Maya kept the envelope in her handbag and then turned towards her mother who gave her a warm embrace. As Maya headed towards the check-in counter, Rajan and Shalini bid her goodbye. They stood watching till they lost sight of her, and then they walked back to their car, hand in hand, in silence. After many years the Malhotra household would be without its sparkle.

As soon as Maya boarded her flight, she opened the envelope and read what her parents had written. Holding the envelope close to her heart, she could smell the familiar fragrance of her mother's perfume. Inside it was a little slice of Maya's childhood. As a nine-year-old, Maya had created beautiful acrylic illustrations of their garden, as a gift for her parents. The painting depicted a serene winter morning, as the sunlight embellished the garden in full bloom. Shalini had carefully preserved the gift as a beautiful token of her love. It was now time to give her the illustrations as a reminder of their love. As Maya turned over the picture, she saw a little handwritten note behind it. Overwhelmed with emotions, Maya began to read.

To our princess,

It fills our hearts with immense pride and joy, as we see you growing into a wonderful, young girl. Each day and moment spent with you, is an enriching and fulfilling experience for us. You have made our lives more meaningful. We have stood together through thick and thin and we promise you our unconditional support, through the rollercoaster of life. As you start a new chapter today, we bless you with all our love. You are a wonderful child and we are fortunate to have you.

Mummy and Papa

P.S. Eat well. Remember to call us every day and use your credit card wisely.

Maya kissed the letter and clasped it to her heart. She had the best parents and she was the luckiest girl in the world. That little handwritten note became her most prized possession for the years to come.

After a long, tiring flight Maya finally reached Dublin—her home for the next four years. The airport was bustling with travellers. Walking out of the terminal, Maya immediately proceeded towards the Air Coach desk. Her college was situated in the centre of Dublin city, approximately 10 km from the airport. Buses departed every fifteen minutes and ferried passengers to the city centre. Maya got her ticket and waited for the next coach to arrive.

It was the month of September and the bronze, burnished autumn leaves covered the parks and driveways. Maya's first impression of the city was downright spellbinding. The eclectic mix of heritage and contemporary lifestyle was extremely intriguing. Dublin seemed to embrace the diversity and multiculturalism of its people. The cobblestoned streets and squares echoed with history and old-world charm.

Maya was awestruck as she stood in the huge, tree-lined, front square. Looking up at the splendid towers of Trinity College, she was about to experience yet another milestone in her life.

The excitement in her voice was palpable whenever she spoke to Rajan and Shalini. 'Put the speaker phone on Mummy, so I don't need to repeat it all to Papa'.

'Okay, okay dear girl. Papa is as excited'

'Yup, Maya, I'm listening.'

'Love you, love you, love you. I'm so happy to be here. It's a complete different form of education. The lectures are supplemented by group tutorials and seminars. The faculty is mind-blowing. I'm learning from the best minds in my field.'

'Slow down, beta, you're talking too fast.'

'Never mind, never mind. Just listen to me... Every student is encouraged to participate in sports, debates, theatre and other social activities, to round us off and prepare us to take on the world after graduation.'

Rajan gave a thumbs up sign to Shalini. 'When are we allowed to come? You've got us all excited as well.'

'When I'm fully settled and can be your guide. Now listen, I haven't finished,' Maya went on, 'the most interesting part of college life, Papa, is the opportunity to interact with people of different ethnic and cultural backgrounds. I know you'll love that. There is so much dignity among us. We all work together with mutual respect and co-operation.'

'That's the only way to be Maya. It not only facilitates cultural integration, but also erases the traditional barriers of religion and nationality. It's an exciting and dynamic world, beta. It will change your perspective towards life and broaden your horizons.' Ranjan was proud of his daughter and happy she had decided on her path with fortitude.

In the first few months, Maya faced minor obstacles with her roommate and adjusting to life away from home. For weeks she kept it to herself, not wanting to worry her parents. Her first troublesome experience was with a girl who had to have the music on while she did her assignments. She ate away at Maya's brains. The second roommate had her phone beeping all night. Maya wanted to stay focussed and had to get her sleep. She finally asked her parents if she could have her own place. Rajan, always the pampering father, indulged her as usual. Maya found herself a studio apartment a mile away from university: a small room with an open kitchen, bathroom and a balcony large enough to fit in a small chair. She sat out at night with her dinner tray on her lap, with a blanket wrapped around her sometimes, aimlessly scanning the beautiful sky or the bevy of people walking merrily out of a nearby pub. She made sure there was an easel in one corner of her room. She painted for hours on Sundays. She now enjoyed splashing earthy colours on her canvas, and landscapes became her favourite subject. In a short time, Maya assimilated with her new environment and made many friends. Her time as a student was as enjoyable as her learning experiences. She also began working part-time for a student volunteering society which organized information and awareness campaigns for social causes.

'Papa I love Trinity College,' she would often say. 'I'm slogging, believe it or not. My goals shall be achieved.'

She had been resurrected like a phoenix—from a confused, aimless teenager to a focussed, mature individual. Law school helped Maya develop her ability to research, coherently analyze and critically evaluate every situation. College life was not only challenging on the personal front, but also intellectually stimulating.

With her hard work and sheer perseverance, Maya got a placement with a community law centre. The internship programme involved research and providing legal support to local NGOs. Her outstanding academic record made her popular with her peers. She actively participated in debates and gave an impressive performance at mock-trial competitions. Maya's life had finally found a sense of purpose.

At the end of the second semester, when Rajan and Shalini visited Dublin, Maya was excited to be their guide around the city. She introduced them to the best local sights and flavours. Dublin was a kaleidoscope of cultures and the local people were extremely warm and gregarious. An old pub and a bottle of Guinness were the perfect start to a conversation or for making new friends. Maya took her parents out for al fresco suppers at the street side cafes. Their most memorable experience was a visit to Wicklow Mountains National park, situated a few miles south of Dublin. Rajan and Shalini were overwhelmed with pride when Maya's teachers and friends spoke admiringly of her achievements and abilities. Maya was a wise and sensible adult now. For the first two years of college, she focussed on developing her core skills and enhancing her positive attributes. She wasn't prepared to settle for anything less than what she deserved. After all the hard work, trials and tribulations, it was her time to rise and shine. She worked relentlessly and pushed herself beyond all limitations.

For every student, the opulent, black-tie ball at Trinity College was undoubtedly the highlight of the year. As a live band belted out their favourite classics, the revellers danced late into the night to celebrate the year gone by. Dressed in a gorgeous, pink and golden dress, Maya looked graceful and elegant. The silhouette of her dress complimented her tall, feminine frame and her long, black tresses fell in a wave over her shoulders. Immersed in the lively rhythm, Maya and her friends danced and swayed in carefree jubilation.

The after-party continued way past midnight, as Maya and her pals left for Cassidy's Pub on Westmoreland Street. The eclectic furniture, incredible music, board games and pictures of comic characters on the walls gave a nice ambience to the place. Every square inch of available space inside the pub was filled with messages, visitors' notes and graffiti. It was one of their favourite places to hang out and down a couple of drinks. Sitting in a cosy corner, sipping craft beer and grooving to their favourite rock and jazz mixes, Maya and her friends were having a glorious time. She was content with the new life she had built for herself.

Defining moments like these were always accompanied by memories of family and home in Delhi. Reclining on her chair, she stared icily out of the window, blankly gazing at the night sky as a gamut of emotions engulfed her heart. How she missed the home-cooked biryani, her favourite chikoo shake, the bird feeder in her balcony and the comfortable leather couch in Rajan's library. A smile escaped her lips as she recalled the time when her father taught her how to ride a bicycle and when her mother had reprimanded her for bringing home a stray pup. How much she loved her parents, how much they had done for her and how grateful she was for their love and thankful for getting an opportunity to educate herself.

Inundated with a heady mix of alcohol and heart-wrenching emotions, maudlin Maya waved goodbye to her friends and lazily walked towards her car. She was frantically searching for the car keys in her handbag as she walked out of Cassidy's.

'Do you need help, young lady?' asked an unfamiliar, husky voice.

Maya turned and took a step back, choking down fear, and blinking against the street light blinding her.

'Madam, you shouldn't make yourself vulnerable to muggers,' the stranger said with a hint of amusement on his face.

The tone was friendly enough for Maya to quickly move to the side and see if he was a fellow student. The smoky eyes behind the square-framed glasses, the mop of dark hair gelled back neatly and the small curve to his lips made a perfect, charming countenance. Rohan was a tall, broad-shouldered man and his confident charm was transcendental. His angelic eyes and immaculate disposition instantly hypnotized her. The South Indian intonation in his voice was pretty apparent. Maya stared at him without blinking, but continued searching the pockets of her bag.

'I guess you are looking for these? You dropped them while walking out of the pub,' he smiled.

Feeling embarrassed, Maya smiled self-consciously and took the keys from him. There was an instant connection between them as Maya stood there staring at him. She then nodded her head, took the keys from him and walked away.

Driving back home, she thought, how could I be such a dolt? I didn't even thank him or ask for his number. It would have been nice to connect with a fellow Indian.

The night was about to fade away and a cup of coffee and her sneaky inclination for a stranger were her companions for the few hours before dawn. Early next day, Maya briskly finished her daily chores and dashed to Westmoreland Street, looking for her mystery man. A clue was all she needed. She knew it was a ludicrous idea, but at that moment she felt like an impulsive teenager.

As soon as she entered Cassidy's, Maya immediately walked towards her corner. She ordered a virgin mojito and dawdled over a magazine. It was so futile to waste my morning, she thought. She looked around and then abruptly spotted a little note scribbled on the window sill.

> *To the gorgeous girl in pink and gold. In case you return to this table and happen to read this... I'd like to say that you are breathtakingly beautiful. I do not believe in social formalities like saying 'thank you', but you can join me for coffee sometime and return the favour.*

Below the text was a funny caricature with square glasses and a number. A crimson hue flushed Maya's cheeks and without any forethought, she hurriedly pulled out her cell phone to dial the number. The butterflies in her stomach fluttered as she waited for him to answer the call. Little did she realize that this handsome newcomer was destined to become a major part of her story.

20

Rohan Narayanan was a management graduate and was working as a strategy consultant with Accenture in Dublin. He had a degree from King's College, London, and came from a wealthy and illustrious family in Chennai.

Maya and Rohan had an uncanny connection. They shared a wonderful comfort zone, right from their first rendezvous at Cassidy's. What followed was a string of coffee dates, shopping trips and movie nights. They enjoyed each other's company and Maya found a great friend and confidante in Rohan. When he was around, she felt the liberty to speak her mind and be herself without any hesitation or fear of being judged. He was well read and had travelled the world extensively. Maya was more impressed by his bookshelves, wit and knowledge, rather than his physical appearance or bank account. A deep philosophical discussion could turn her on more than expensive gifts or romantic dinner dates. Rohan also stood by her in times of distress and Maya felt emotionally secure in the relationship. He fuelled Maya's confidence to kick-start her own social venture the minute she finished her degree. Maya was sure he was the brightest bulb in her life. Every time they were apart, he strayed into her thoughts and she would feel a pulsating love for him deep in her bones. He was her Mr Perfect.

One afternoon Maya wanted to surprise Rohan and bake a cake for him. She felt her feminine, motherly side come out around him. She had helped her mother in the kitchen occasionally during her adolescence. She stepped out of her door with a spring in her walk and a smile on her lips. Putting the ingredients together, she happily hummed her favourite song, 'Strangers in the Night'. Halfway through her very ambitious cake, Rosaline, her friend from college called seeking help for an important assignment. Maya, animatedly chatting over the phone, added double the quantity of flour prescribed. Her cake went into the oven and came out looking flawless. Their candlelight dinner at home was perfect too.

'I have a surprise for you,' Maya said after dinner and dashed off to the fridge. 'With all my love, Rohan, I've baked this for you.'

Rohan, impressed with his surprise, lifted her off the floor and cuddled her in his lap.

'You are a dream girl. Good at everything you do.'

They held the knife together and tried slicing the cake. Alas! It was as hard as a rock.

'Don't worry, love, I have a brilliant idea. Maybe we can hammer it down and use it as doorstopper. All your effort won't go waste.'

He carried Maya in his arms to the sofa and hugged

her tightly. 'I love you in spite of your lousy baking. Let's get cake from the bakery near campus tomorrow.'

Maya burst out laughing, 'No way. I have to get the cake right. You are invited for dinner again tomorrow and I promise you'll end up eating the whole damn thing.'

Their light-hearted banter kept their equation balanced, and no argument ever spiralled into any serious altercation. Was their relationship for real? Maya often wondered.

As the winter semester drew to an end, Maya requested Rohan to accompany her on a trip to Delhi. The Malhotra family was going to visit Udaipur for the wedding of Rajan's nephew. Rohan now an integral part of Maya's life. She desperately wanted to introduce him to her parents. Although there had been no fancy proposal with flowers or a diamond ring, Maya and Rohan were sure they wanted to spend their lives together. For her, he was the perfect companion, mentor and friend. They could spend hours in a library, walk together on the banks of the Liffey under the moonlit sky, or just spend the night on the terrace with a bottle of wine. She always spoke about him at length while talking to her parents. Shalini was impatiently biding her time to meet her future son-in-law. Rohan took two weeks off from office and decided to join Maya on her Indian sojourn.

The fortnight was packed with celebrations and merriment. Maya introduced her 'friend' to her family and cousins with much pride. Rajan and Shalini were delighted to see Maya happy. The bond between them was evident. The Malhotras asked Rohan if they could meet his parents and formalize their relationship. Maya was overjoyed at her parent's approval.

There were several occasions when Maya felt a strong urge to share her life story with Rohan. She did not want to keep any secrets from him, but her insecurities always held her back. She had grown tremendously as an individual, with strength, focus and foresight. But somehow, Maya had not been able to come to terms with her inner self. Her soul felt entangled at times by her past. Rohan had to be taken into confidence. It would be unethical to hide something so crucial. She turned to her father for advice. Rajan encouraged her to tell him.

A few days later after dinner Maya poured her heart out to him.

'Rohan, I need you to know I am an adopted child.' She was upfront. Rohan blinked several times, unable to fathom for a second what she had just said.

'Honey, I'll be back in a second. I'm just a little thirsty,' he stood up, fondled her hair with a smile, and went to pour himself a glass of water.

He had to digest what she had just announced. His expression was unreadable. He was a sensible man and was not going to reveal he had been stunned. He poured the water slowly and Maya's eyes studied him, trying to pick up any signs of astonishment. She played with her hair, pushing it back several times. Rohan walked back to her, pulled her up from the sofa and gave her a tight hug and kissed the corner of her mouth.

'It doesn't matter to me, honey. All I see is a beautiful, accomplished girl standing in front of me.'

Maya held back her tears. 'I have deep gratitude for my parents. I know my birth mother would never have been able to place me where I am today, but sometimes I feel incomplete and want to know why she gave me away. On my birthdays I feel weird. Everyone around me had nothing to do with my birth. So many friends have told me I don't look like my parents and I don't like hearing that.'

Her throat was dry. She had so much to discuss but today was not the day. All she wanted was for Rohan and his parents to know she was actually, not a Malhotra.

'It's no big deal. I understand resolving your birth issues can be a problem. Don't ever vilify your birth mother. Maybe she had her compulsions. You don't know her reasons, honey,' Rohan said.

It was important for Maya to be tranquil with her reality and stay happy.

'No point digging into a chapter of your life which isn't relevant anymore, Maya,' Rohan reminded her.

'But I want to know.'

'Maybe one day, we will,' Rohan pulled her up and sat her on his lap. 'There's a time for everything.'

He kissed her eyes gently. She buried her head on his neck and cried.

Maya had heard innumerable stories and anecdotes about Rohan's childhood, his school friends and his ancestral home in Chennai. Rohan had grown up in a big joint family with his grandparents, uncles, aunts and cousins. The Narayanans were an orthodox family and religiously followed their age-old customs and traditions. For three generations, their family had been actively involved in state politics and commanded enormous power and influence in the area. Maya's excitement to meet them was coupled with anxiety and apprehension. After all, their families were poles apart.

Rohan's father, Mr Venkat Narayanan, was the regional Member of Parliament of the ruling political party in Chennai. Their family had immense clout in their social and political circle. Maya and her parents were amazed to see a fleet of cars waiting outside the airport to escort them to Rohan's ancestral villa in Adyar. The Malhotras were graciously welcomed with lavish arrangements and fanfare. Rohan's grandmother greeted them with a traditional aarti and vermillion on their foreheads. Rohan swelled with pride as he introduced Maya to his family and took her around the palatial villa. Like a little child, he couldn't stop babbling about his childhood memories, his favourite toys and the summer afternoons spent with cousins playing badminton. The passion and elation in his voice was so infectious that Maya couldn't help but listen with rapt attention. She had never seen this facet of his personality, and was amused to see the strong, independent Rohan transform into a 'mama's boy'.

The three-day trip to Chennai was eventful, filled with city tours, shopping and lavish family dinners. However, the most significant moment arrived, when Maya and Rohan visited the Kapaleeshwarar Temple with their families. Standing in the temple courtyard, amidst the holy chants, hymns and the lingering aroma of incense sticks, the two families decided to consecrate their relationship. Rajan and Shalini were ecstatic as they blessed their darling daughter for a blissful new phase in her life.

Maya still had to finish her college degree and Rohan had work commitments in Dublin. Hence, the families decided to have an engagement ceremony before the two went back to Ireland. There was no time to send invitations or make elaborate arrangements, so they had a small family affair to celebrate the occasion. Maya, dressed in a traditional silk sari, looked ethereal with a string of flowers adorning her hair. A family pandit conducted the ceremony and blessed the couple for a prosperous life ahead. As a token of love, Rohan's mother gifted a beautiful necklace to welcome Maya into their family. The gem-studded necklace was a family heirloom that had been passed down for generations. Maya felt honoured to receive it. She revelled in these moments of joy. She felt like a Diwali sparkler had illuminated every part of her being.

As the couple sought blessings from their elders, Maya had an absurd urge to share this moment with Gita aunty and Jagdish uncle. She hadn't seen them in years, but their unadulterated love was still as fresh as the morning prayer in her mind. Dewy eyed, she looked at her mother standing next to her and found solace in her arms.

The two-week vacation had finally come to an end and it was time to fly back. Boarding their flight to Dublin, Maya and Rohan walked in unison, bidding adieu to her parents and looking forward to their journey together.

21

Maya was now in her final semester. She had been working diligently on her research project and had received great acclaim for her social work. Her keen interest in international politics, world affairs and social issues helped in honing her skills as a lawyer and social activist. There was a sea of opportunities before her.

Back home in India, Rajan and Shalini were busy making preparations for a grand wedding celebration. While Maya wanted to have a traditional ceremony at the temple, Rohan's family insisted on having an ornate ceremony in both cities. Rohan was their only son and heir to their political legacy. A never-ending list of guests was prepared, including family, friends, political bigwigs, industrialists, socialites and celebrities. From designer outfits and royal invitation cards to the finest decor, the Narayanans made sure their son's wedding became an affair to remember. Rohan's mother, Sunanda, personally monitored every little detail of the arrangements.

Maya and Rohan landed in Delhi just a week before the ceremonies were to begin. The Malhotra mansion was bustling with energy and Maya was delighted to be back home. More than trousseau-shopping and catching up with friends, Maya rejoiced in the little moments she shared with her family. She assisted Shalini in making laddoos, packing gifts for their relatives and sprucing up the house. She would often spend the evenings with Rajan, discussing her future plans over a cup of hot chocolate. Rajan admired her zeal and was extremely proud of his little daughter. Like a little sapling, they had nurtured Maya for years, and today it was time for her to blossom. Her confidence and newfound bliss filled their hearts with joy.

On the wedding day, as the priest chanted shlokas before the holy fire, Maya and Rohan looked into each other's eyes and promised themselves to each other. The festivities continued for six days, with different ceremonies for both Punjabi and Tamil traditions. It was a beautiful amalgamation of rituals and cultures. The guests were treated to a delectable spread, from sumptuous chicken tikka to rasam and idlis, along with exotic fruits and mouth-watering desserts. With fanfare, festivity, abundant blessings and teary eyes, Rajan and Shalini gave their daughter away and wished her a blissful, married life.

Maya and Rohan had been living together for two months before they were united in matrimony. Their relationship wasn't just about sharing the same bedroom or being physically intimate. It was about sharing their lives, through all the highs and lows. From grocery shopping to preparing breakfast and doing the laundry together; they cherished every moment together. A mutual respect for each other's private space and work commitments was crucial for a modern-day couple living in a cosmopolitan society. Both Maya and Rohan complimented each other perfectly, like blocks of a puzzle. Reading books, watching movies, walking down O'Connell Bridge or just sipping coffee and cuddling under the sheets, Maya and Rohan found magic in the simplest of moments spent together.

A week after their wedding, the newly married Narayanans had to rush back to Dublin as Rohan had some urgent work commitments. Maya's final semester was over and her next priority was to establish her own social welfare organization. Through her work experience with several NGOs and state-run organizations over the past year, she had built a team of like-minded, young professionals and volunteers. She wanted to pursue a master's degree, develop her professional identity and work with community groups at the ground level. Rohan, on the other hand, was going great guns at his job. He had been offered a placement in New York, but his ultimate aim was to start his own enterprise. Despite the long working hours and hectic schedules, Maya and Rohan always tried to spend quality time together. Weekend getaways were the perfect way to rejuvenate. Life was moving in the right direction, but the circumstances were about to take an unforeseen turn.

Eight months into their wedding, Rohan's father suffered a cardiac arrest and they had to immediately rush back to Chennai. It was a difficult time for the family, as Mr Narayanan had been the force behind the family's social, political and financial responsibilities. Sunanda's role in the household had been restricted to family matters and in this hour of crisis, Rohan had to stand by them. Like a dutiful son, he took a break from work to go back home. He had been living abroad since the age of sixteen and it took him some time to learn the intricacies of their family business. The work culture in India was very different and it was harrowing to acclimatize to the new environment so suddenly. Another major burden on Rohan's shoulders was to carry forward the political legacy of his father. The party supporters and cadre looked up to him as the successor. Through this period of turmoil, Maya stood by him like an anchor. She kept travelling between Chennai and Dublin, making all efforts to be with her new family and manage her work and studies simultaneously.

Months passed but the storm refused to settle down. The unrelenting pressure of work and family responsibilities started picking at their relationship. Maya felt alienated at times, as she tried to juggle between two worlds. It was difficult being a supportive wife and a dutiful daughter-in-law at the same time. Besides travelling between two continents, the pressure of her own work was more then she could handle.

Slowly Maya conceded that their relationship wasn't working out. The Narayanan family was extremely orthodox and traditional. The women of the family were confined to their duties in the kitchen and there was no acceptance for independent expression of ideas. Their culture was completely different: the food, language, customs and lifestyle. Life looked worse when Maya began to notice a change in Rohan's behaviour. The pressure made him unreasonably aggressive and Maya had to bear the brunt of his anger. Their conversations would often end up in fierce arguments. As an independent, educated and modern woman, it was difficult for her to give up her own identity. She craved for a few moments of togetherness and missed their lives together in Dublin. As much as she understood Rohan's plight and wanted to stand by him, the growing friction between them only made it worse.

One evening Maya coaxed Rohan to accompany her to the local Barista. It was crucial to step out of the family home and spend some time alone. On the table by the window, Maya and Rohan sat opposite each other, avoiding any eye contact. The growing friction and Rohan's indifference was easily discernible. After a few minutes of painful silence, Maya looked him in the eye, placed both her hands on the table, leaned forward and decided to confront the issue head on.

'I understand it is a difficult time for the family and it is our responsibility to stand firmly by their side,' said Maya, as her voice choked with emotions. 'But it's been three months now and Appa is recovering well, by the grace of God. This might seem like a selfish decision, but you need to move back to Dublin so we can be together.' Tears streamed down her cheeks, as she covered her face with a tissue.

Rohan instantly crossed over to her and wrapped her in a warm embrace. He had failed to understand her misery or appreciate her selfless efforts. But now it was time to make amends and start afresh. He too wanted their marriage to work. After a long deliberation, Rohan and Maya made the decision to fly back to Ireland two weeks later. Rohan's decision to take a sabbatical from work had cost him dearly, as he had lost his promotion to a junior colleague. Back in Dublin, he perennially worried about his family and went to Chennai every month. Every time he returned home, Maya could sense the growing distance between them. She immersed herself in her research to keep herself occupied. Rohan, on the other hand, could not strike a balance. His mind was being tugged in two different directions.

A few months later, at a seminar entitled 'Social Activism and Modern Political Intervention', Maya was offered a new field placement and internship under a United Nations programme. It was a lucrative opportunity for her to establish herself professionally and connect with community leaders. It was time to translate her academic training into a profession. She was supremely excited about the new opportunity and its possibilities. As part of the internship, she had been assigned to work for a community outreach programme in Peru and Equador. Thrilled by the prospect, Maya rushed home that evening to surprise Rohan with a candle-lit supper.

The aroma of scented candles, a perfectly laid dinner table and Rohan's favourite payasam made the perfect setting. Excited, Maya rushed to open the door as soon as she heard Rohan's car outside. Standing at the front door, dressed in an elegant peach dress, Maya welcomed him with an affectionate embrace. Popping a bottle of Chardonnay, she handed him the letter of appointment. Rohan blankly stared at the letter and sat down on the sofa without saying a word.

'I thought you would be really happy…' Maya trailed off as she knelt on the floor and held his hand close to her chest. That night, as she looked into Rohan's eyes, a foreboding silence engulfed the room.

All these years, Rohan had been the wind beneath her wings. He had stood by her, inspired and encouraged her through the highs and lows. He had mentored her wisely. But sadly, their circumstances were driving them apart. Maya had given him endless chances, even when he had faltered. But finally today, she surrendered. This was another blow to her.

Why did people close to her always neglect her? Her mother's tyranny, along with Rohan's indifference haunted her. She slinked into her room without a word and lay down curled up in foetal position.

Rohan was consumed by the urge to move back to India and take over his family business. With his father's ailing health, he had also been unanimously chosen as his political successor. But Maya could not give up her work and life, and live in a conservative joint family. She had not worked so hard just to be a housewife doing mundane, obligatory chores every day.

This agony had been simmering inside her for over a year and was now ready to boil over. This was a battle of priorities and she had to put her foot down. As much as she loved Rohan and understood his predicament, she knew that she could not give up her own. She could not sidetrack her career when Rohan could not meet her halfway.

Over the next few weeks, the growing distance between them translated into an awkward silence whenever Rohan came back from work. They had decided to sleep in separate rooms. Maya would serve him dinner and return to her room without a word. She immersed herself in her work and dissociated herself completely from her friends and social circle. She was in no mood to be around people. It was a difficult time for both of them: a time to introspect and find answers. The long drives, coffee dates and movie nights were replaced by a stoic silence and discomfiture. The promises of a lifetime seemed to be fading away.

One afternoon when Rohan was in office, Maya received a parcel in his name. Just as she was about to place it on Rohan's desk, she noticed the name of a law firm in Chennai. It was marked as 'Urgent and Confidential'. Maya was curious. After much deliberation, she opened it. Inside the box was a copy of the memorandum for registration of a consultancy firm in Chennai. The detailed paperwork, permissions, investment reports and bank statements revealed that Rohan had been planning to shift back home for a while, without her knowledge. Maya was dumbstruck.

When had Rohan become so insensitive, keeping such a huge decision a secret from her? Tears streamed down her cheeks and her colour turned ashen. Maya realized their story was over.

Rohan and Maya had always been each other's anchors. They shared every little detail of their lives, discussed the smallest issues and worked in unison as true life partners. But times change, and so do people. Maya realized that it was time to walk away, with her head held high, in order to respect the dignity of their relationship and cherish what they had shared together. Her resolve to put away the negativity and file for a mutual separation was a decision she took with a heavy heart.

She had never spoken about their marital discord with her parents, so the news of their divorce came as a shock for Rajan and Shalini. They tried to persuade her to give themselves a bit of time to settle down, or maybe give themselves another chance. But Maya was firm. She could not be herself or achieve her true potential if she carried on with a relationship which had frayed. Dignity and self-respect were two emotions her parents had taught her to cherish from a very young age.

Speaking to Shalini over the phone, it was easy for Maya to open up and request her parents to respect her decision. 'Mummy, I hope you will understand me. When a connection starts to fade away, it creates a vacuum which is quickly filled up by negative emotions. Rohan and I have shared love, trust and dignity. They were the foundation of our relationship. I understand Rohan's quandary, but sadly, our priorities are driving us in different directions.'

Rajan and Shalini were deeply concerned about their daughter. But as always, they were going to stand by her under any circumstances. Shalini immediately booked their tickets to Dublin to make sure they were with her during this time. The separation was mutual, but painful. There were days when she felt upbeat and there were days when she felt lost. There was no magical cure and she had to hold on till the tsunami would pass.

Maya was a strong, spirited woman like her Nani. Rather than sulking, or feeling resentful, she channelized her energy into productive work. She knew she could clear all her obstacles and emerge once again as a woman of substance. This was a harrowing time for Maya, not just because of the emotional turmoil, but also the financial constraints that came with a separation. Paying the EMIs for her car, the tuition fees for her degree and renting a new apartment was challenging. Her father often offered her assistance, but Maya refused.

She was an adult with a good education and learning how to support herself was the very least she could do. She took up freelance assignments, worked overtime and never shied away from odd jobs at the local supermarket in order to make ends meet. For all the events that unfolded—the sleepless nights, moments of loneliness, the highs and lows—Maya learnt to love herself, completely and unapologetically.

Maya's parents became her anchor in the storm. She could confide in them, vent her angst and cry on the phone, appreciating that they would always love her without being judgemental. These fraught times helped her evolve as an individual. She found solace in the little pleasures of life: meandering in the cobblestoned streets of Dublin, enjoying the sunsets and the quaint seaside. She worked tirelessly to realize her dreams and make a mark as a social activist. She used her qualifications as a lawyer to provide legal assistance to underprivileged families and refugees. Her internship with the United Nations earned her great acclaim and experience. Over the next two years, she travelled extensively for work and started her own social reform and awareness organization. As part of the programme, she provided culturally appropriate services for indigenous communities and fought against discrimination. Maya also actively participated in various legal education conferences and community awareness forums.

Every evening when she returned to her apartment she felt a sense of fulfilment and pride. She had created a cosy reading corner in the living room and decorated it with little planters, wind chimes and origami butterflies, comforting objects from her childhood,. The leather couch by the window was her favourite place to relax. It reminded her of the warmth and comfort of her father's library. A small, mahogany treasure chest, filled with her sketches and artwork was right next to the couch. A cup of hot chocolate and her favourite novels kept her company when no one was around. Maya was never lonely. She felt liberated and content. Her trials and tribulations taught her valuable life lessons and gradually strengthened her into the person she was meant to become.

22

Back home in India, the past had suddenly returned to the present. Ganesh had come back to Delhi after twenty-five years to exorcise the ghosts of the past. Gita and Jagdish had not heard of him after he had deserted Mamta. For Ranju, he had disappeared the day she walked him to the auto to go back to his village.

From meagre beginnings, Ganesh had now created a successful farming collaborative in Bengal. His son lived in Kolkata and handled their business there. He had coaxed Parvati into organic farming before his return from Delhi. It was a relatively new concept for the villagers at the time. But the growing demand for organic produce in the big cities made it a lucrative opportunity. Ganesh had a strong networking ability and business acumen. Along with his hard work and years of experience, he had won the trust and support of the farmers in his village and the neighbouring villages. Their company now sourced large quantities of organic produce and dairy products from the villagers and sold it to big dealers in Kolkata after processing and packaging.

Ganesh was in Delhi for a trade fair for organic

agricultural produce. He saw it as a great opportunity to educate himself further about the business. There were presentations on livestock breeding, agricultural machinery, replenishing soil fertility and tapping new markets. It seemed to be a promising platform to showcase his company's products and connect with new dealers.

The Kolkata Rajdhani Express arrived at New Delhi Railway Station at nine am. Ganesh stepped out of the train and struggled to push away the memories he had banished to a corner of his heart. This city had given him love and companionship. His love for Mamta was timeless, although he had done the unforgivable. He pined for the intimacy that he had shared with her. He ached to see Mamta and Ranju again, even if only from a distance. Walking through the crowded platform, overwhelmed by the bittersweet memories, Ganesh was remorseful about his unspeakable act all those years ago. He had loved Ranju, but a moment of madness had ruined everything forever.

He walked out of the station and stood there in silence, looking up at the sky as the crisp winter breeze sent a chill down his spine. The agro-trade fair, a three-day event, was being held at Pragati Maidan. Ganesh had booked himself a room near the station.

It was a chilly winter morning and there was plenty of time at hand. Ganesh asked the autorickshaw driver to stop at a tea stall on the way. Unable to quell his restlessness, he immediately lit a cigarette and took a long drag. He sat down on a cemented bench outside the stall and stared at the people passing by.

'Papa!' said a little girl standing behind him.

Ganesh swiftly turned around with a dumbfound expression. His emotional state was getting the better of him. Right behind him stood a 5-year-old girl, holding on to her father's hand. Her big, brown eyes lit up with joy as she looked at the candy-filled jars and freshly fried jalebis.

'Can I have some of these?' she pleaded with her father.

Ganesh felt an inexplicable anxiety ran through his veins. His urge to see Mamta and Ranju overpowered him. He just had to see if they were alright. How would he confront them? What could he say? How was he going to justify his absence for all these years? A million questions hovered in his mind, but Ganesh did not have any answers. The demons of his past had tortured him for all these years. But now, it was time to face them and find closure. He immediately stood up, sat in the auto and said, 'DID Colony.'

The city of Delhi had completely transformed over the years. A maze of flyovers now dotted the skyline. However, despite the development and urbanization, Ganesh also witnessed the growing inequality. The luxurious, upmarket shopping malls, grand and impressive, were juxtaposed with slum settlements and scores of homeless people on the footpaths.

With a foreboding uneasiness etched on his countenance, Ganesh alighted from the auto at the road leading to DID Colony. Coming back from work, every evening, he recalled how he and Mamta had walked together through those narrow alleys. Contrary to the outside world, nothing had changed in here. Ganesh was transported back in time. Walking past the neem tree, the putrid stink of the open drains zoomed into Ganesh's nostrils and racked his stomach. He looked around at the little children playing cricket and his eyes frantically searched for Mamta. The thick, winter fog veiled him from the neighbours. Walking towards Mamta's shanty, Ganesh trembled with anxiety. Their misfortune rested on his shoulders, but the urge to bundle Mamta in his arms and fly her away to another planet was there too.

Standing outside the shanty, he looked around apprehensively and hoped that Mamta had forgiven him. He knocked hesitantly at the door. After two minutes of deafening silence, he heard the sound of approaching footsteps and waited in anticipation. However, to his surprise and consternation, he saw Gita standing at the door. Dressed in an off-white saree, Gita's dark billowy hair had turned silver and she looked frail and old. She stood at the door, unable to recognize Ganesh. His shuffling gait, wrinkled forehead, thick glasses and sparse, grey hair was a stark contrast to the attractive, striking persona of his youth. After a few moments of awkward silence, Ganesh mumbled who he was and tried to peep inside the shanty to catch a glimpse of Mamta or Ranju.

Gita's forlorn expression quickly changed to angst and repugnance. She had always disapproved of Ganesh's proximity with Mamta, and his sudden disappearance had only confirmed her suspicions. Now he was back.

For what? Gita had been witness to all that Mamta had endured. If she had any inkling that Ganesh was responsible for the most horrific chapter of Ranju's life, she would not have even allowed him into their shanty and handed him over to the police. Even without knowing the full truth, twenty-five years was a long time and no excuse could have justified Ganesh abandoning her best friend. Gita had the right to demand an explanation.

Sitting on the foldable bed, Ganesh stared at the ground in utter dismay as Gita narrated the events that had unfolded all those years ago. With tears streaming down his face, he could hardly contain his anguish. The gravity of his offence was beyond justification and any repentance could not diminish the burden on his conscience. Without a social certificate of matrimony, Ganesh and Mamta had lived like a family. But today, Ganesh held the moral culpability for all their misery and hardships. Like a strong woman, Mamta had fought till her last breath to support her family despite all social and financial constraints. Ganesh could not even fathom the adversities and anguish faced by Ranju, who lived with the trauma of being raped and the stigma of being an unwed mother at a young age. In his single moment of weakness, he had scarred so many lives forever. There was no atonement for his sin.

Gita then filled him in about her own life. Five years ago, Jagdish had passed away after a chronic illness, and ever since then, Gita and Ranju had lived together in Mamta's small shanty. Gita's family had grown and had moved away to Ghaziabad. Ranju continued to work for Mrs Banerjee during the day, looking after her household duties and taking care of her. Thereafter she would come back to the shanty to look after Gita aunty. She had finally come to terms with her adversity. In the evenings after work, she would often attend sewing lessons with the girls in the neighbourhood. Through the years Ranju had never bothered to ask where her daughter was. This was a conscious decision to dissociate herself from her past. Time could not wash away the scars on her soul. She had been stripped of her dignity, innocence and pride. She still didn't trust people or build relationships and hence, never married or desired a family of her own. Life had a way of crushing dreams and disrupting plans.

Ganesh was filled with remorse when he heard about Maya. The little child, bereft of her mother's love, had been given away to another family. Gita had no information about the Malhotras, despite Ganesh's repeated requests. 'We just hope and pray that she is happy in her new world. Besides I don't know where she is!' she exclaimed. 'For her birthday every year we just visit the temple and pray for her wellbeing.'

Overcome with shame, Ganesh was speechless. Nothing that he could say or do would ever amend anyone's life. With a guilt-ridden conscience and a heavy heart he offered to provide financial help for Ranju, but Gita blankly refused.

'Mamta was a strong, independent woman and would never approve of this,' she said, looking at Mamta's picture hanging on the wall.

Penitent and aghast, Ganesh decided to leave the shanty and never come back again. The damage he had caused was irreparable and he had to live with his disgrace forever.

Few years after her divorce from Rohan, Maya decided to move out of Dublin and shift her work base to London. Her organization collaborated with numerous social activist groups and communities across Europe. Like mature individuals, Rohan and Maya had buried their differences, and their friendship had triumphed over all bitterness. Rohan had moved back to Chennai and was working hard to strengthen his new enterprise and carry forward his father's legacy. In times of emotional distress or confusion, Maya often called him to seek advice and assurance. He continued to be her mentor.

During one of her work meetings in London, Maya bumped into a college mate at a seminar. Samina, a graduate in social work from Trinity, had opened a retirement home for the destitute and elderly. Revisiting their college days, Maya and Samina spent the whole afternoon together.

'Your story is impressive, Samina. I'd love to visit your retirement home when convenient.'

'Super, please come and share some love and cheer,' said Samina. 'Bring along some fruits and don't shy away if you sense an air of desolation. The vagaries of old age are etched on to the wrinkled faces and the pain of loneliness is evident in their eyes. It's sad, but some of the residents have been abandoned by their children, some others had been found on footpaths.'

'I'm proud of you, dear friend. You are providing love, care and appropriate medical supervision for the destitute and homeless, so they can spend their old age peacefully and have a dignified end. You are a true humanitarian,' Maya patted Samina's back.

At Samina's retirement centre the following week, Maya exclaimed, 'How cruel children and families can be! It's wonderful to see that you have created a joyous environment, conducive to their emotional wellbeing.'

Sitting in the garden, during their circle time, Maya watched the residents sharing their stories and funny anecdotes. She and Samina joined in the laughter after everyone had danced, rejoiced and devoured the cupcakes Maya had brought along, like little kids in a candy store.

'The helium balloons and cotton candies might have seemed like a strange idea,' Maya carried on laughing, 'but the smiles and laughter tell a different story.'

'Bringing a smile to someone's face is easy, and is the most rewarding gift, Maya. I've learnt with time to be a giver, even if it's just a smile or a flower,' Samina said as Maya nodded.

As Maya walked towards the door, an old army veteran came up to her and handed her a little pouch with his unsteady hand. 'What is this?' she asked politely.

'It's a badge I received from my commander, when I left the army. Keep it as a token of our love and blessings. You are a wonderful soul and we thank you for these precious moments of joy.'

Maya eyes welled up as she hugged him.

As the sun set and the skies turned black Maya crawled into her bed and then dragged herself out a little while later. Walking up and down her living room, she couldn't get over the time spent at the old age home. It had, without a doubt, changed her perspective towards life.

She held her head in her hand and felt guilty about harbouring a strong animosity against her mother. All of Maya's accolades and achievements seemed meaningless that night. Pulling herself together, she resolved to go back to her parents in Delhi and find Ranju. It was time to mend a broken bond and start afresh.

23

Harmony and stability are the most vital ingredients for a peaceful life. For Maya, the last few years had been extremely fulfilling, but there was a missing link between her and her happiness. But now, it was time to let go of the bitterness and pain that she had harboured all her life, and evolve into a compassionate human being. She had never ever given any thought to going back to her roots or figuring out why her mother was the way she was. The sudden need to understand the reasons behind her terrible actions kept pricking at Maya's consciousness. She couldn't contain herself.

Immediately she called Rohan and spilled her guts to him.

'Yes,' he said to her, 'wait for the right time.'

In some corner of her heart, she instinctively knew why Rohan had decided to go back to his family and stand by his mother. Separated by circumstances, Maya and Rohan were still united in spirit. After sharing her experience at the retirement home, Maya finally gathered the courage to reveal her closely-guarded secret and her present dilemma.

'All these years, I have been struggling to find answers and come to terms with my own identity. As a 5-year-old child, it was difficult for me to accept the apathy and indifference of an irresponsible mother. She gave me up for adoption, and the agony of being an abandoned and unloved child pricked at my soul. She was cruel and hated me. I wonder why? I need to know. I need closure. Through these years, I was so consumed by my own perplexity that I even failed to appreciate the selfless affection of those who embraced me with open arms. I took my parents for granted as well. But now it is time to reciprocate all the love and unwavering support that I have received all these years.'

Maya was unsure how Rohan would react, but he promised to stand by her.

'Maya, life often places us in situations where we feel confused. But standing at the crossroads, each one of us needs to focus on our ultimate destination and choose our path wisely. I think you should do what you have to do. You have wonderful parents and they will respect your decision and always stand by you. The time has come.'

Two months later, Maya finally packed her bags and bid adieu to London. Dublin and London had given her the best years of her life: from the carefree days of college to the heartache and sleepless nights of romance and marriage, along with the hard work she had put into building up her organization.

When she touched down at Delhi airport, Maya's parents were waiting for her with a bunch of her favourite white carnations. Throwing her bags down, she ran and hugged them tightly. 'I'm so happy to be back home to the best parents in the world!'

On the drive back home Maya sat between her parents, holding their hands affectionately. Shalini couldn't resist showering her with hugs and kisses. 'At last you are home, my darling.' The Malhotra mansion had once again been elaborately dressed up to celebrate Maya's homecoming. Her bedroom door had strings of marigold flowers hanging from the door frame and the balcony was lit up with white fairy lights. A collage of her old photographs hung on the walls, recalling the memories of her beautiful childhood. Rajan had recreated a small reading corner for Maya, with a collection of old and new books lining the mahogany shelves, along with Maya's favourite leather chair from his own library. As the family sat down for dinner that night, Rajan couldn't help but notice Maya's disquietude.

'Let's go for a little stroll after dinner and we can have some ice cream in the Malcha Marg market.'

Walking arm in arm with her father, Maya refused to meet his gaze.

'Is everything alright, my girl?' Rajan asked, lighting a cigarette.

Maya could barely contain her emotions. 'Yes, there is something I need to talk to you both about and I will, when the time is right. Nothing to worry about though,' she said and held tightly to her father's arm.

Without a single word, Rajan kissed her forehead and rubbed her back. For Maya it was a silent reassurance that her parents would always be her greatest strength. She had every desire to take them into confidence, but Maya first had to face Ranju and wash away the angst for her biological mother. Besides, she never wanted her parents to feel she was ungrateful and feared they might be hurt.

A week later, Rohan flew down from Chennai to give Maya moral support, and thus began their journey to retrace Maya's past. She was capable of locating Ranju on her own. Maya was no stranger to the streets and alleys leading to her shanty. DID colony was en route to Gymkhana Club and Maya had passed it by thousands of times. She could have stopped to check on Gita and Jagdish but the discomfort in her stomach and the ghastly memories of her mother stopped her all these years. Rohan turned up early at Maya's doorstep and together they left for DID Colony. They parked the car at a distance and walked down the street. The neighbours and passersby stared at them with curiosity.

Maya's eyes kept searching for a familiar face in the crowd. Her stomach somersaulted a zillion times and her turbulence was transparent. Maya walked past the neem tree with caution. How could she ever erase this neem tree from her memory? Wasn't her Nani's corpse placed under this very neem tree? It was under this tree that her mother had shoved her aside as she wept over her Nani's dead body. It was this very tree under which she sat for hours, waiting for her Nani to return home from work. This neem tree was etched in her memory like a permanent wound.

Maya gritted her teeth and wiped her face. A weariness settled on her brow as she pulled up her cotton sleeve and stopped in her tracks. She had to feel good about what she was doing, otherwise there was no point. She had to expunge all her adverse feelings and centre her thoughts. She was anxious to find out about her past and accept why she had been abandoned.

What caused her mother to treat her so shabbily?

As Rohan stopped to take the bottle of water out of his backpack, he suddenly realized that Maya had to finish this journey on her own and walked back to the car. Maya kept walking towards the shanty, searching for her mother.

Right outside the cluster of huts was a little elevated platform where the slum kids were playing with marbles. Right there, standing under the street light, was Gita aunty. Maya was unsure till she saw her limp towards the huts. She straightened her back and confidently walked up to her, stood in front of her and bowed down to touch her feet.

Gita was startled. There had never been any communication from Mrs Banerjee about Maya, and they had lost all hope of ever seeing her again. As Maya introduced herself, Gita stared at her in disbelief and then wailed like a hungry baby. Their little girl with dreamy eyes had magically transformed into a charming, beautiful and confident woman.

Gita welcomed Maya into the shanty with a humble treat of samosas and tea. Her hunched back and wrinkled face spoke volumes of her pitiable condition. Inside her shanty, nothing much had changed besides a fresh coat of paint. The heat was unbearable.

'The electricity has not been there since early morning. They are putting new cables for the ministers house,' Gita said while handing out a paper fan to Maya.

With dewy eyes, Maya looked around at the soiled kitchen utensils in the corner and clothes hanging on a line to dry.

Life was extremely tough for the people in the shanty. The pittance they earned was never enough to live a decent life. Ranju still worked as a housemaid with Mrs Banerjee, and earned just about enough to sustain their household expenses. Gita's children worked in Ghaziabad and sent them a fraction of their salaries, all of which was swallowed up by Gita's medical bills.

Ranju wasn't home that morning. Mrs Banerjee was down with an acute viral infection and Ranju was staying with her for a few days. As Gita narrated the story of their hardships and Mamta's inimitable spirit, Maya was greatly inspired by her Nani's resilience. Her picture on the wall was covered with a thick layer of dust. Maya immediately stood up to wipe it clean with her scarf. The millions of unanswered questions which had been crushing her soul suddenly dissolved into thin air. Recollecting the horrific incident that scarred Ranju and brought Maya into their lives, Gita burst into tears. She held on to the foldable bed to support her fragile frame. Maya looked around for Rohan, but she knew he was allowing her to spend time with Gita aunty alone.

Just as the morning sun breaks through the fog, Gita's words washed away all the misunderstandings and agony in Maya's heart. She could understand the predicament of her mother, who was raped at a tender age and then forced to bear the child. One incident had totally ruined her life and stripped her of a better future.

There was nothing she could do to alleviate her pain or change the past, but Maya vowed to ensure a better life for Ranju and Gita aunty. With folded hands, she humbly expressed her wish to buy them a new home, where they could comfortably spend the autumn of their lives. After much persuasion Gita nodded, unsure if Ranju would accept Maya's offer.

She discouraged Maya from meeting Ranju. There was no point in raking up painful memories. There were still days when Ranju relived her agony. Maya respected this sentiment, content to let both of them live in peace.

Ranju and Gita aunty moved into a three-bedroom flat in Ghaziabad, near Gita's children. At Maya's behest, Mrs Banerjee had gifted the house keys to Ranju. 'Let it be a gift from you, Mrs Banerjee,' Maya had told her. 'A gift acknowledging her countless years of service.'

Maya also made arrangements for Ranju to receive her month's salary as a pension. She had finally come to terms with an intensely disturbing chapter of her life. It was not easy.

'Mummy, I went to DID Colony to meet my birth mother. Please don't look at me like that, I just had to. I struggled with this for many years and the time had come for me to know everything about myself. It was important. I couldn't brush it under the carpet anymore. It was the right time. You and Papa don't need to worry about a thing. I didn't get to meet my birth mother but I met Gita aunty, my Nani's best friend. I'm feeling better about myself and relieved, now that I know the circumstances of my birth and why my birth mother was the way she was,' Maya finished in a rush.

Shalini was unnerved and Rajan was quiet. But Maya handled her parents with composure and kindness.

'Mummy, you are the only mother I have. But I had to find out for myself and accept who I really am.'

The wound which had been festering for so long had finally healed. With abundant love, appropriate guidance and a good education, a little girl from the slums had blossomed into a beautiful woman with confidence, dignity and poise.

Acknowledgements

My sincere appreciation to my publisher and editor for shaping the book and accommodating my last-minute changes. Thank you also for producing a cover better than I had imagined. A big thanks to old buddy Ranjan Kapoor for making the time to take my photo. Last but not the least, I would like to thank my interlocutors, the subjects of this book, for patiently answering my innumerable questions and never failing to offer me a cup of tea and biscuits.

Indoo Seth is the author of two novels, *Emotional Hostage* and *Love Laws & Outlaws*. She writes women-centric stories enveloped in romance. Before she started writing, she was a successful entrepreneur. She has been on the Central Board of Film Certification (Delhi State) for two years.

When she isn't writing she is doing yoga, dancing, walking, gardening, gymming and travelling.